*Murder
at the
Friendship Hotel*

By Charlotte Epstein

Murder at the Friendship Hotel
Murder in China

Murder
at the
Friendship Hotel

CHARLOTTE EPSTEIN

A CRIME CLUB BOOK
DOUBLEDAY
New York London Toronto Sydney Auckland

A Crime Club Book
PUBLISHED BY DOUBLEDAY
a division of Bantam Doubleday Dell Publishing Group, Inc.
666 Fifth Avenue, New York, New York 10103

DOUBLEDAY and the portrayal of a man
with a gun are trademarks of Doubleday,
a division of Bantam Doubleday Dell
Publishing Group, Inc.

Library of Congress Cataloging-in-Publication Data
Epstein, Charlotte.
        Murder at the Friendship Hotel / Charlotte Epstein. —1st ed.
            p.   cm.
        "A Crime Club novel."
        I. Title.
        PS3555.P645M86   1991
        813'.54—dc20   90-49976
                                                                           CIP

ISBN 0-385-41708-X
Copyright © 1991 by Charlotte Epstein
All Rights Reserved
Printed in the United States of America
May 1991
First Edition

10 9 8 7 6 5 4 3 2 1

FOR PAULETTE
WHOSE CREATIVE INGREDIENTS
HELPED THICKEN THE PLOT

*Murder
at the
Friendship Hotel*

One

WELL, SHE'D DONE IT AGAIN, Janet sighed. Like one of her own students putting off for another year what she would have to face sooner or later. The kids backpacked around Europe or joined the Peace Corps, promising themselves that the year or two away from school would make them better students when they were ready to get back to finishing college; she always thought it was harder for them to settle down once they had known the freedom and excitement of being on their own. Would she ever be able to settle into academic life and try to make some sense of it?

Here she was back in China again at the first invitation that seemed to justify asking for another leave from the university. They would never have let her go just to teach English again. Though she had loved her year preparing Chinese scientists in English so they could go abroad to study, she had to admit she was somewhat overqualified for that job.

But setting up a Department of English in a new university— that was fine with the starched-collar-and-tie crowd at home. They'd have another plum to incorporate into their advertising campaign: Professor Janet Eldine, prize-winning author, scholar, recipient of honors and awards—now *internationally* acclaimed— could teach anywhere; but she chooses to be part of the faculty at Kirktown. She'd join the long list of famous people to choose Kirktown. The last one was a stand-up comic who'd "chosen" the only college he could afford when he got out of high school, and who hadn't stayed long enough to get his degree. But the ads never mentioned that.

It was good to see old friends again while she waited in Peking for her trip to Huhehot in Inner Mongolia where the new university was being established, financed jointly by American business people and the Chinese government. It was hoped that the site would make it known as a center for higher education of minorities—groups identified officially here as "nationalities." She would be starting from scratch, selecting faculty and developing programs. It was an exciting prospect. Maybe if she was in on the ground floor of a new school she could keep it from becoming the dreary, unhappy place that Kirktown was.

Sometimes she felt that it was Kirktown University that had stood between her and Daniel.* Struggling against the arbitrary administrative decisions, the lowering of standards, the meanness and backbiting among competing faculty had left her no resources for dealing with the searing questions that separated them. Perhaps distance would give her perspective—and Daniel too. After she returned from her two years in Huhehot they might try again to close the breach, to be for each other what they both needed.

As she sat this afternoon, her attention wandering back and forth between the book on her lap, her thoughts of home and the anticipation of the upcoming trip to Huhehot, someone knocked at her door and waited for her to open. Not a Chinese, then: they knocked and opened immediately.

She was pleased to see Dorothy Gault, hand raised to knock again. Definitely not Chinese. English. Sturdy, solid, country English, with the complexion of a fresh tea rose. Dorothy finished getting into her cardigan while she talked. "Let's catch the bus to Wangfujing," she said. "It's a great day for getting your ribs punctured."

Janet grinned and grabbed a jacket. "Just what I was thinking. Maybe we can pick up some chocolates in town."

"I don't know how you stay so thin—all the chocolates you eat."

* *Murder By Law.*

"I worry about it. That keeps me thin."

"There's a best-seller diet book in that somewhere," Dorothy laughed. "Let's go."

They ran down the stairs of Yo Yi Ping Guan—the Friendship Hotel—and followed the winding path past the building of shops and the recreation hall to the bus that was ready to leave. Residents and workers at the hotel could ride the bus to town, once in the morning and once in the afternoon, for only five fen. It was a marvelous convenience, not having to use the unbelievably crowded public buses.

Dorothy's reference to punctured ribs was not about the bus; it was on Wangfujing, the main shopping street where people came from everywhere, that one risked being gored. That was how most Chinese people made their way through crowds—by elbowing others out of the way.

But, elbowing aside, Janet loved Wangfujing. In the shops people gathered around whenever she approached a counter, eager to see what she bought. In the street people stared and called hello. Small children toddled up to grasp her legs and teenagers stopped her to practice an English sentence they had learned in school.

Now she and Dorothy walked along looking at shopwindows, crossing the street to a stand selling Cokes and orange drink. Suddenly, in front of them, a tall young woman gave a small surprised grunt and pitched forward into the crowd. Hands reached out to keep her from falling but she was propelled through a gap in the crush of people and fell in front of the only car that was likely to pass there within the next few hours. There was a blaring honk and a sudden silence as the horn cut off.

Janet and Dorothy got to her in time to see the car's passenger kneeling at the woman's side, his hands passing over her very intimately. Her eyes were squeezed shut as if in anticipation of catastrophe. Slowly she opened them.

The man's hands were gentle, feeling her arms, her legs, her ribs. One hand went under her, to the back of her head, her neck, down her back, and Janet could see her suppress a giggle.

"Nothing broken," he said. "Can you get up?"

She put her arms around his neck and let him help her. They

stood for a moment very close together, then slowly she let her arms move to her sides. She nodded and murmured something— perhaps "Thank you."

Dorothy found her voice. "Are you all right? Goodness, you could have been killed!"

"I think not." The deep voice of the man was brisk. "We were just crawling through the crowd."

"I'm fine. I can't imagine how I found room to fall."

"It takes some practice walking on Wangfujing," he said. "You must learn to resist the pushing with counterpressure." He looked at her seriously but his eyes laughed. "Would you like to sit for a few minutes?"

"Yes, please."

He helped her into the back of the car. No one seemed to mind that it remained in the middle of the road. Those people who didn't stop to watch and discuss what was happening just parted like the sea and flowed on either side of the vehicle on to their destinations.

"You're Ian Chen, aren't you?" Janet had to look a long way up to him. "I remember seeing you at the welcoming ceremonies for foreign scientists several years ago."

He nodded. "I recognize you too. I once heard you speak about the effects of overcrowding on group attitudes. Important stuff. Are you all foreign experts?"

"Yes. Carol is teaching English at Beijing Xue Yuan. Dorothy teaches English literature at Beijing University, and I'm on my way to a new university in Huhehot. Carol is the one you knocked down."

He smiled and turned to stoop at the car door. "How do you feel?"

"Fine. I'll get out now. Thanks for your help."

"Maybe you'd better drive her back to the Friendship Hotel," Janet suggested.

"No, no, Janet. That's not necessary." She was out of the car and on her way. "Thanks again," she said over her shoulder.

Janet smiled vaguely to Dr. Chen and walked after her. "Hey, wait up."

Dorothy had been uncharacteristically silent. Now she also caught up with Carol and slowed her down with a restraining hand on her arm. "What's the matter with you?" she demanded. "Why are you running from him?" Her eyes sparkled with excitement.

"I'm not. It's just all so embarrassing. Forget it, will you?" She bent once to brush ineffectually at her skirt as they walked.

"Isn't he gorgeous? He's a Yank, I think. A doctor. I've seen him around the hotel. Do you think he's staying at the Friendship Hotel? I've seen him there once or twice. Janet, answer me! Where do you think he's staying?"

"I've seen him going into one of the apartment houses across the compound from the hotel. I read that he's been invited to work in the lab at Bei Da." Bei Da was short for Beijing Daxue, Beijing University. "They're trying to develop a pill for men. Genetic engineering too. You know—population control."

"He's rather a famous man in America. I didn't realize he was so tall."

The non sequitur startled them into silence. Janet suppressed a grin at herself. She found him a very attractive man, even if she *was* twenty years his senior. She focused consciously on more intellectual matters. "He's very interesting—" she started to say.

"He certainly is!" Dorothy exclaimed.

"No, I don't mean that. I mean his attitude toward the work he's doing. Here's a man who's made great discoveries in contraception, yet he makes speeches against population control."

"That doesn't make sense."

"It does when you hear him. He says population control programs of the type China has wouldn't be necessary if we weren't locked into national boundaries. It's population dispersal and food distribution that ought to be worked on, not better contraception and abortion."

"Then why does he do what he's doing?" Carol asked.

"Well, I think what he says is that effective contraception is needed in the short run, because the real problems will take much longer to solve. They say he's brilliant. There was talk of the Nobel—"

"I hope you didn't miss the only opportunity you'll have!" Dorothy broke in.

"I don't think so," Carol answered, as if she was certain of something. Then she looked startled at her own observation. It didn't seem to square with her running from him. Maybe it related to the way he had looked at her and to the way her arms had been clasped behind his head. The other women eyed her thoughtfully.

They reached the department store and began picking their way through the dozens of men, women and children squatting on the wide pavement in front of it—resting, waiting to start home, or just people-watching. On the second floor Carol pointed to the counter selling cotton coats, those softly quilted garments that had found their way to the West. Ian Chen stood there chatting amiably with the clerk, fingering one of the gray coats.

"I'd like to get one of those for a friend back home," Carol said.

"Well, come along," Dorothy answered enthusiastically. "He apparently speaks Chinese. He'll be able to translate for you."

"No," Carol said, pulling back. "Not now. I want to buy a pair of shoes first. China is the only place that has shoes small enough to fit me."

"What is it?" The Englishwoman was exasperated. "You're behaving like a schoolgirl, or as if you don't like him. That kind of man is rare in Beijing, especially one who speaks our language. Or, at least, yours," she added, reviving an old joke about Americans not speaking English.

He looked up and caught sight of them, and turned from the counter to wait for them to reach him.

"Carol wants to buy one of these for a friend in the States, but none of us speaks Chinese."

He looked gravely at Carol, waiting to hear what she had to say for herself.

"Please don't bother about us," Carol said coolly. "I can make myself understood well enough to get what I want."

He took her at her word and turned back to the counter. Not rudely, just acknowledging her wish.

A second clerk came up and Carol pointed to a coat on display.

For a moment he stared at her bright red hair and her face with the startling turquoise-colored eyes. No Chinese could fail to catch his breath at this alien vision. The linen jacket she wore must have been carefully chosen to match those eyes. Janet wondered how long she had searched the shops to find just that shade of turquoise.

Accustomed to being stared at, she motioned to the clerk that she wanted a larger size, and when it was brought out from behind the counter mentally measured it against her friend. But only half her mind seemed to be involved in the transaction.

She took the ticket from the clerk and went over to the cashier to pay and get her package. Dorothy was trying to give her meaningful looks—to do what? Stay and make awkward conversation? Dawdle so they could move out of the store together?

"Dorothy," Janet said when the three women were back on the sidewalk, "you're acting silly. What the hell has got into you?"

Dorothy drew a deep breath and seemed to sober suddenly. "My God, I don't know. All I can think of is that we mustn't let him get away. Don't you two feel anything?" she asked curiously.

Carol's fair skin telegraphed her feelings to the world as her face flushed.

"You do! You feel it too!"

"He's very attractive. But so what? He's not the first good-looking man I've ever seen."

"Oh no, you won't get off with that. He's not just good-looking. He's something else . . . I can't quite . . . quite . . ." Her voice faded away as she struggled to find the words for what she was feeling. "What did you say?"

"Wh . . . ? Nothing."

"Yes. You said trust. Trust. That's it."

Carol tried to answer practically. "All right, so he impresses me as the kind of man you can trust. But that's only a first impression. How can we tell what he's like from a moment's conversation?"

"Trust," Dorothy repeated, as if she hadn't heard the rest. "That's what I never had in my two husbands. That's what was always missing. I was never sure that I was safe with them, that I could be myself."

"Well, don't rush to marry this one before you find out a little more about him," Janet advised her.

"Go on, kid about it. Just because you didn't feel it."

"But I did. Don't let the white hair fool you."

"It doesn't. Did you know your eyes change when you talk about him? They go from cool green to a sort of greenish gold."

"Sure you're not just seeing your own reflection in them?"

Janet felt a light pressure on her elbow moving her through the people sitting on the ground. He had come out of the store and was apparently heading for his car, taking it for granted that they were too. As they walked he bent toward Carol and murmured, "Would you like to see a two-thousand-year-old Buddhist temple?"

She looked askance at him without answering, pretending to be absorbed in negotiating the terrain. The driver started the car as they approached, and Chen handed Dorothy, Janet and Carol's package into the back seat. "The driver will deliver you to the Friendship Hotel," he said.

Janet's last sight was of Carol's startled eyes and open mouth as she was smoothly bustled away.

Two

THE NEXT DAY Carol couldn't wait to tell Janet all about her evening with Ian Chen. First she had phoned Dorothy, and now she was in Janet's room talking while Janet, wrapped in a robe, sat sleepy-eyed but attentive.

When the story was barely begun Dorothy came in, still fastening her skirt. "You promised you wouldn't start without me," she said breathlessly.

Carol went on: Ian had held her hand as he led her along Wangfujing and down a less crowded side street, as if she were a small child or a comfortable lover. What was she doing following a total stranger down foreign streets where she couldn't even ask for directions if she needed to get back alone? Normally she was infinitely more cautious than this.

As they went away from the center of the city and began to leave the shops behind, people stared at the foreigners even more openly. Her bright jacket and red hair were enough to attract attention in a world of dull blues and grays. And though Dr. Chen was obviously of Asian background, his sharply creased cords and plaid shirt immediately identified him as a Westerner. The staring was not as cheerful as it was on Wangfujing. No one called hello, and children were not encouraged to approach them. Foreigners did not often find their way to these streets.

They passed small ancient stone houses that had been damaged by time and the earthquake of thirteen years before. Although they were patched picturesquely with odd bits of wood and metal, they must have been hell to live in during the heat and bitter cold of the changing seasons. Now, in the early fall sunshine, most of the family life was going on out of doors: a grandmother running after a bare-bottomed toddler, a man having his hair cut, a woman washing cabbage leaves in a tin pan under a crude tap.

They did not speak as they walked, both of them absorbed in the life of the city—the real life, not the ambience of foreigners and tourists to which she had become accustomed. Their long legs kept pace effortlessly and as they strode through the ancient narrow streets she thought they must have looked ten feet tall to the people who lived there, shining creatures from another world. They could hear the silence fall as they passed, and the chatter start up behind them.

Carol became aware that Ian was looking at her and she wondered what her face had been mirroring of her thoughts. Her love of China? Her fascination with Chinese customs? Her feeling that she could spend her life here, with the overwhelming dissatisfactions and abrupt departures of the past finally over for her?

They came suddenly onto a wide, unpaved square. Rising from the center of it was a two-tiered pagoda etched against the clear blue sky in a harmony that almost sang. The fluted blue roofs touched the heavens in testimony to the symbiosis of men and gods and gave Carol a sense of peace she had never known before.

"What is it?" she whispered.

He had looked slowly away from the structure to her face, and his own softened. "You feel it too," he said. "I knew you would."

("The Temple of Heaven," Janet whispered, remembering the first time she had seen it.)

Carol and Ian had stood there for a long time before turning away. The harmonious perfection of the temple had flowed into them and made them suddenly one.

(Janet almost regretted that her own experience had not been quite so lovingly shared. Dorothy only pursed her mouth in a soundless whistle.)

A sharp elbow in her side had jolted Carol back to solid ground. They were among the crowds again and it was hard to believe in the serenity of the temple such a short distance away. The moment she smelled the odor of roasting chicken coming from Beijing's equivalent of a fast-food stand, she had announced, "I'm starved." That should completely break the spell, she said to herself.

But it didn't—not altogether—because he looked at her for a moment, startled, then laughed aloud. People around them stared. She grinned at him ruefully. Was he laughing because he had read her mind? Could he tell that she was having a hard time keeping her natural wariness alive? He had put his arm around her shoulders and hugged her to him as if he understood all too well, and hustled her along. "What do you think," he finally asked her, "of eating Peking duck in Peking?"

They made their way through small streets, some unpaved and flanked by very old houses, each with a wall around it, others where new concrete apartment houses were going up. If ever there was a symbol of China, Carol had thought, it was the wall. Almost every hovel, every temple, every government building was surrounded by a wall. The metaphor intrigued her. Were the people too surrounded by psychological walls, reluctant to lend themselves to life with foreigners? As friendly as the Chinese were, through every Chinese day ran the theme of caution against foreigners. The *People's Daily*, the only and official Chinese-language newspaper, warned of the dangers of being seduced by Western philosophy: criminals roamed the streets of American cities and money was the ruling god of the West. Although it was important for the welfare of China to learn Western technology, they must be on guard against absorbing Western decadence. She hoped that those Chinese, like Ian's family, who had in generations past migrated to Western countries had not inherited the psychological walls. The warm, strong hand that held hers seemed to promise that they had not.

The restaurant looked like a family home with each room set up for dining. They were greeted in a small foyer by a man dressed in the usual gray trousers and white, short-sleeved shirt. He appeared put out for a moment when Ian spoke to him but, like a true entrepreneur anywhere in the world, he recovered his aplomb immediately and led them to a small table in the main dining room rather than to one of the rooms at the back where foreigners were usually seated. The conversation of the other diners was stilled for only a moment, but even when it started up again the curious looks did not stop.

"Duck?" he asked her.

She smiled and nodded. "Everything," she answered.

He laughed and ordered. It was a long time before the dishes started to come, but then they seemed never to end. Duck and hoisin sauce and pancakes to roll them in; lotus hearts fried in a delicate batter; dofu in a pepper sauce that burned the roof of her mouth and that she loved; slivers of pork in black bean sauce that made her close her eyes in ecstasy.

"A mixture of cuisines," Ian had explained. "Some of the cooks here are from the north, some from the south. I told them to bring everything."

When they started to leave, Carol went on, half a dozen waiters as well as the proprietor lined up to bow them out. Then, from a large table around which sat about fifteen young people tightly packed, one got up and came toward them, blocking their way out. Some of those seated near him tried to stop him, reaching out hands that he brushed aside, hissing words he ignored.

He stood, feet apart, hands behind his back, leaning toward Ian Chen, and spoke in a low, intense voice. The proprietor began to shout and several of the waiters grabbed him, but they couldn't budge him or make him stop talking.

As he listened, Ian's face had taken on a stony look but he made no move to answer or to leave. Finally the man finished what he had to say and with a satisfied smile bowed ironically and went back to his friends. Ian took Carol's elbow and steered her through the aisle of tables and out of the door. There was no sound in the restaurant; everyone stared at them, some open-mouthed in horror, others blank-faced. On some faces Carol thought she could see a faint smirk of gratification.

They walked quickly back to the main street while Ian's face gradually softened a little. After a while she risked asking him what the incident was all about. At first he tried to shrug the whole thing off by saying the man was just drunk and didn't know what he was saying. But then he shook his head. "No, it wasn't only that," he said. "Oh, he was drunk all right, but he knew what he wanted to say. He accused me of betraying China."

"How?"

"He said the research I was doing was a fraud, that I had no intention of providing anything useful for China's program. That I was prolonging the research and sabotaging it and preventing honest Chinese scientists from making discoveries that would save China."

"Do you know the man?"

"No, I don't think I've ever seen him before. He accused me of being in cahoots with . . . with . . ."

"With whom?"

He shook his head. "No, it's ridiculous. There's nothing in it. An isolated nutcase."

"You've never heard anything like this from anyone else?"

"No. Let's forget it, shall we? Don't let it spoil a beautiful evening."

Carol had said nothing more and they linked arms and sauntered down the street, stopped to look over the shoulders of four men squatting under a streetlight playing cards. There were still many people around, all of them talking, and so at home did she feel with this man that she forgot that the talk was in Chinese and that she didn't understand a word. At the door of the hotel he had asked to see her again.

"Did he ever say whom he was supposed to be in cahoots with?" Janet asked her.

"Not exactly. But he said he had an invitation to dinner from two good friends, Mark and Mary Allen. Do you know that name?"

"Mary Allen? Isn't she the writer, the one who does all those articles against birth control and abortion?"

"That's right! I thought I'd heard the name before. Well, he said she was his very good friend."

"Do you think that man in the restaurant meant Mary Allen? That he was plotting with her to destroy his own research?"

"Crazy, isn't it?"

"I don't know. People do crazy things."

"Oh, but not Ian Chen. He's the most sane person I've met in a long time. He told me something about his boyhood and I was really touched."

"I grew up in Seattle," he had told her. "My father took us there when the attacks began in San Francisco, the attacks against the Japanese. He didn't want to put up a sign saying 'I'm Chinese, not Japanese.' It was not only personally humiliating; by implication it denigrated another group. We were a loving family, my sister, my father, my mother."

"Now," demanded Carol, "would a man with that kind of background be so dishonest as to devote his life to defrauding two governments?"

Janet murmured some assurance to her friend and avoided suggesting that there were more variations of human perfidy in the world than she had ever dreamed of.

"What *two* governments?" Dorothy asked.

"Well, he gets a lot of his research money from U.S. Government grants. Most of that money goes into his laboratory installations at home. But they're all working on the same thing."

"I don't believe any of it. It's too devious. He's a gorgeous man and you mustn't let him go."

Carol needed someone calm and levelheaded to reflect back her own enthusiasm. She was falling in love with a stranger and she knew how dangerous that was. She wanted Janet's good sense to raise practical questions, but without throwing cold water on her feelings. She also wanted Dorothy's cynicism to make her laugh at herself, but without spoiling the romance of the affair.

"Dorothy, what would I do without you?" Her beautiful smile lit up her face. But, she reminded herself, I'm never impulsive in my relationships. Love with a stranger? Nonsense!

Janet smiled too, but then asked: "Did he say anything about his friendship with Mary Allen? Explain how two people so diametrically opposite in philosophy could be good friends?"

"We didn't talk about her. He asked me to dinner tomorrow night so I could meet her. Her husband is arriving then."

"Oh, good. Then you'll be able to judge for yourself."

"I hope so," Carol said doubtfully. "I'd hate to think . . ."

Janet hoped, for her sake, that there was nothing to the accusation of the man in the restaurant.

Three

LATER THAT MORNING Ching Fu Gen, chairman of the Department of Foreign Languages at Beijing Xue Yuan, where Janet had taught English, met her at the door of the college and greeted her as an old friend.

Another tall Chinese, Janet thought. And he wasn't even born in the vitamin-packed United States. People who thought all Chinese were short had obviously never been to China.

"Come in, come in, Professor!" He led her to his office and offered her a chair, the same kind of chair that furnished her hotel room. There was no time or energy to spare on varying the production of necessities. Efforts were reserved for increasing quantities rather than introducing creative variations.

She smiled at the warmth of his welcome. He seemed like a shy man, modestly dressed like a Chinese worker. But she knew this was just the surface Ching Fu Gen. In reality he was an influential administrator and scholar whose suggestions for changes in higher education were more often than not instituted merely on his say-so.

"You are comfortable at the Friendship Hotel?" he asked her.

"Yes, very comfortable. Thank you for arranging it for me. It's really more than I expected."

"We want you to be happy in China. You come here to help us and we are grateful to you."

"You're very kind, Mr. Ching. It's good to be back again."

"You like China." He grinned ingenuously. The Chinese were never tired of hearing that foreigners liked their country, their food, their ancient temples.

"Yes, very much." She smiled back at him.

"We will go to Miss Walker's class soon." Both he and Carol had insisted that she sit in on Carol's English class. "The students know you are coming. They have heard much about the American professor who taught here three years ago. They know that almost all your students passed the examinations."

"Oh, that wasn't my doing, Mr. Ching. They all worked very hard to learn English."

The Chinese students she had taught were so different from American college students. It was not only that they had been carefully taught to respect teachers and to appreciate their dedication to knowledge and learning. They were also very easy in their respect, not always on guard against some perception of threatening authority. The key to their attitude, she thought, was that they really wanted to learn.

It was true that they saw their education in very practical terms, knowing that the more they learned the more likely they were to get the jobs they wanted. American college students also wanted jobs, but they were not convinced that knowledge and learning were what they needed to succeed: the diploma was their goal, the symbol of learning rather than the real thing. And, preferably, a diploma from a prestigious school. It was all symbol in the United States. In China it was all knowledge and skill. That was their reality in a world where they were committed to making enormous progress in modernization. She respected Chinese students as much as they respected her. It had made her feel good about teaching in China, even if she was teaching English and not the subject she had qualified in. But there had not been much call for teachers of psychology in the China of three years ago.

"When the class is finished, I would like to invite you to come with us," Mr. Ching was saying. "You will be interested."

She smiled in anticipation. When she had been a teacher here no one ever "invited" her to come anywhere; she was just told five minutes before the event that an outing had been arranged. It had taken her some time to accept what she felt was presumption on the part of the college authorities. But she had to admit that the trips were usually fun.

"A very famous scientist is at Beijing University. From your country. It would be useful for the students to hear him speak, especially as he speaks in English. He will be here today to lecture and then we will visit his laboratory at the university."

"I hope he'll make himself understood. It's early in the year and they haven't been studying long."

"Oh, we will have a translator to help, of course."

"Of course." She suppressed a shudder. The official translators in the college all spoke English "a little." They had been largely self-taught, with their study topped up by Chinese teachers of English. Their English skills were very, very limited.

"But I understand that this scientist also is fluent in Chinese. He will be able to make himself clear, I am sure. You will be pleased to meet someone from the U.S.," he said as if he was certain. "Although he is Chinese," he added.

"Yes, of course. I'd love to come along." She noticed that he didn't call the Chinese-American scientist her countryman. The Chinese were somewhat conflicted about Americans of Chinese ancestry. They called them overseas Chinese and, although they didn't trust them any more than they did other foreigners, they often treated them in the same proprietary manner they used with their own people. The worst of both worlds, she thought. "I think I've met this scientist," she said. "Is his name Ian Chen?"

"Yes, yes. Dr. Ian Chen. He will be happy to see you again. And then this evening we will have a banquet in his honor. And in yours too, and Miss Walker's. For the help you all give to China and to our students. We will go to a restaurant in the city. It will be very good, you will see. In your honor. In the scientist's honor."

Chinese banquets were delicious affairs. She didn't know about the honor, but the food was something to look forward to.

When Janet and Ching came into the classroom Carol was talking to the students gathered around her. Janet saw Wang Qu Qing and waved to him. Three years before, he had been a bright undergraduate in the college, self-taught in English and Russian and doing his rebellious best to ruin his future. He did not appear to have mellowed at all since his graduation. Curiously, in spite of the need to reprimand him repeatedly for associating with foreigners, for insisting that everyone call him Quentin (his way of Anglicizing his name), even for wearing jeans, he had been appointed to the staff as a junior teacher of English instead of being shipped off to some backwater province to practice his own profession, engineering research.

The period had not yet started. Carol looked up and greeted Janet. Mr. Ching introduced her and the students' response was flatteringly cordial. Apparently they really had heard about her. After a few minutes she took a seat at the back of the room and Ching returned to his office. She wondered how Carol felt about Ian Chen's coming to lecture, but she didn't have a chance to ask her.

It was a four-hour class with ten-minute breaks at the end of each hour. About ten minutes into the third hour, Ching Fu Gen came back with Ian Chen. Carol stopped speaking in the middle of a sentence and stood there staring at them, a flush moving quickly up her neck to her face. Janet laughed to herself. So they were still doing the same thing. No one had bothered to prepare Carol for Ian's visit. The poor woman was so flummoxed that she acknowledged Ching's introduction automatically, unable to say quickly enough that they had already met. Janet, from the back of the room, could see Ian's exaggerated deadpan as he shook Carol's hand. She went forward to say hello and to give Carol a chance to pull herself together.

Once he started the lecture, Ian was all business. He described his ideas of how genetic engineering could not only control population numbers but also manage the production of desirable sex ratios and the elimination of genetically determined disabilities. It was a calm and thoughtful presentation by a scientist who was soberly cognizant of the responsibility he had taken on. He must be very brave, she thought, to do this kind of work. The whole idea scared her to death.

Wang Qu Qing sat at the back of the room hanging on Ian's

every word. When Ian asked for questions, Qu Qing raised his hand. "I have decided to study biochemistry," he announced. "You have shown me what I must do." True to the way he seemed to order his life more for shock value to the cadres than any sensible plan for his own success and happiness, he was impulsively switching his field of study again. Well, if anyone could do it, he could.

"Come and see me when you're ready," Ian told him. "Maybe I can be of help to you."

The principal would feel like killing his junior lecturer when he heard about this. That would please Qu Qing immensely.

"Yes, Dr. Eldine? You have a question?"

"I was wondering," Janet said slowly, "if you've encountered much resistance to your research in the United States." She didn't want to be contentious but she thought the Chinese scientists needed to know that there were other points of view besides their own. They themselves were so completely committed to population control and genetic engineering that they never considered that the whole area of research had very vocal opponents in other parts of the world.

"Yes," Ian was saying. "There are those who are afraid of the power men assume for themselves when they begin to change the conditions for birth—and death. Suddenly we have all kinds of information and technology at our fingertips and the power they give us is almost overwhelming. Some people think we shouldn't use it at all, regardless of the consequences. Others think we must use it all and let it carry us as far as possible, again regardless of the consequences."

"And you, Dr. Chen?" Carol asked in a low voice. "What do you believe?"

He looked at her for a long time, knowing that the question was not only for the education of her students. "I think," he began deliberately, "that there are dangers inherent in genetic engineering. Those who have the knowledge and skill may begin to believe that they have the right to decide what kind of people should be born and what kind should be prevented from being born. Although knowledge does convey a certain power, that power should never accompany the absolute right to use it. Decisions in this area should never be left to the experts."

Later, Janet told Dorothy about his answer. "I wonder if he wasn't being just a little too rational."

"You don't believe he's committed to what he's doing?" Dorothy asked.

"He's so clear about the potential dangers, he sounds almost uneasy about letting them loose in the world."

"Maybe he's just that—a rational man who can see all sides of an issue."

"Could be. But I've seen some of Mary Allen's writing. It's vitriolic. If writing can be violent . . ."

"Against his kind of work?"

"She thinks it's immoral. Curious basis for friendship, isn't it?"

Four

BEFORE IAN LEFT he told Carol that arrangements had been made for her class to visit his laboratory after lunch. No one had bothered to mention it to her. She didn't know either that there would be a banquet for the three foreigners after the lab visit. She took the surprises more calmly than Janet ever had when she was teaching at the college. This sort of thing used to drive her crazy.

On the way back to the Friendship Hotel they shared the car. Carol was very quiet and Janet wondered what she was thinking about with such intensity. As they were getting out of the car Dorothy came down the steps of the building next door where she had her rooms.

"Hello, you two," she greeted them. "Have a good morning?"

"Do you think I could risk having my hair done at the hotel beauty shop?"

"And a good afternoon to you too!" Dorothy laughed.

"Huh? Oh, sorry. Hi, Dorothy. Do you?"

"Well, it's a risk. You have a choice of having your hair evenly chopped all around; that's the latest style for Beijing glamor girls. Or you can have a perm—all squiggly rolls that get frizzy even in the dry air of Beijing."

"Oh, give me a break." She sat down absent-mindedly on the bench at the foot of the steps and the others sat with her.

"Don't tell me you feel a sudden need to dazzle all your little bookworms! I don't think they'd notice if you came bald to class.

They would still follow you around as if you were the Pied Piper of Hamelin," Dorothy teased.

"They're just desperate to pass the exams. They want to get every bit of information they can." Like most good teachers, Carol didn't like the insinuation that she was making the students too dependent on her.

"Are you sure they're not lusting after you as any sensible man would? No, no. I retract that. The Chinese do not lust. They work, they study, they concentrate on right thinking. How do you suppose they manage even that one child each couple is allowed?"

"So much concern with sex before lunch," Janet observed mildly. "What's turned you on?"

"A dear friend is coming to visit me! I can't wait to see him. It will be wonderful to have a man in my bed again."

Janet laughed and Carol chuckled ruefully as if it was not so simple and uncomplicated for her.

"Is he someone you love, Dorothy?" she asked.

"Remember the poem?" Dorothy struck a pose and recited airily:

> Out upon it, I have loved
> Three whole days together!
> And am like to love three more,
> If it prove fair weather.

"Not love then?"

"John Peter is a dear but I settle for pleasure, friendship and even—occasionally—joy. Love, at least the kind of love we've been brought up to expect, is an illusion. The mass media will have a lot to answer for on Judgment Day!"

Carol smiled uncertainly and rose and the three women walked up the stairs without talking. Carol made a vague pass at her hair.

"Wish I had hair like yours," Dorothy said. "It's like silk and satin. It turns up at the ends as if you'd spent hours on it."

"You think it will be all right?"

"All right for what? Hey, what's up?"

"It's Ian Chen. He's invited my students to visit his lab and then there's a banquet tonight."

"Ah, Ian Chen. I'd do some primping for him myself."

"Be serious, can't you?"

"I am serious. John Peter will be here for a very short time. Then he'll be gone and I will make my lone way again through a thousand million Chinese, and not one for me."

Carol shook her head in mock exasperation.

"That's your problem: you're too serious. What's more important—Ian Chen, getting your hair done, or the fact that they have cheese in the hotel store today?"

"Cheese," Carol repeated blankly.

"Cheese!" Janet yelled.

"Yes, cheese! Has it occurred to you that you haven't had a bit of cheese since you got to China a month ago?" she asked Carol. "Once in a great while they get some in for foreigners and there's a great rush on. You'd better get over there within the next half hour before everyone gets back from work and hears about it."

Carol nodded. "Cheese," she repeated, as if she had never heard the word before. She left the other women and turned to her own door, opened it and went in. She didn't hear Dorothy say something about "dotty Americans." Or Janet's retort: "Glass houses."

After Janet had freshened up she knocked at Carol's door to remind her about lunch. Reluctantly the younger woman agreed to eat. There really wasn't time to fuss with her appearance.

The car was waiting for them when they left the dining room. They stopped at the college to pick up Mr. Ching and Mr. Cai, the principal, and were driven to the campus of Beijing University where they pulled up at a new cement-block building.

Inside Janet looked around the large room filled with tables at which white-coated men and women sat at microscopes and test tubes. The students had already arrived and were crowded in the back of the laboratory. Wang Qu Qing, the brilliant rebel, had also come along.

"I didn't realize so many people were working on this. There must be about a hundred—"

She heard Carol's indrawn breath and followed her gaze to the man coming toward them. Ian Chen had heard her comment.

"There are seventy-five scientists and three times as many lab assistants. And this is just one installation. There are a number of them around the country."

"Yes, I should have known. In a labor-intensive country like China any priority program would have more than enough people. And population control is certainly a priority program."

"Unfortunately!"

Janet turned, startled. The gray-haired woman who had moved to stand beside them, listening openly to their conversation, had spoken forcefully, almost angrily. She was a Westerner, not one of the students, and she carried a notebook and pencil. A reporter? Before anyone could reply, Mr. Ching had her by the elbow and was trying to move her back toward the door. Ian Chen intervened. "It's all right, Mr. Ching," he said, putting a restraining hand on the other man's shoulder. "Mrs. Allen is here at my invitation."

"Mrs. Allen," Mr. Ching said grimly, "is not friendly to China. She does not understand—"

"But she is still a guest of China, isn't she, Mr. Ching?" he asked quietly. Mr. Ching's arm dropped to his side. "I thought Mrs. Allen should have an opportunity to see the work about which she has such strong opinions."

"The students are here," Ching protested. "I do not think they would be interested in those opinions."

"How can you tell?" He smiled to take the sting of rebuke from his words and shrugged as he turned to walk to the front of the room. "Let them argue with the lady and learn from the argument."

Ching shook his head in disagreement. He was afraid it might only weaken their belief in the program if they listened to what he was convinced were the wrong answers. He could not believe that exposure to all sides of an issue could help students arrive at the best possible answers. As far as he was concerned, others had already arrived at the only possible answers and those were the ones the students should be given. Educators were forever confusing indoctrination with education.

Dr. Chen gave an overview of the total program and then focused on what was happening in this laboratory. Mrs. Allen seemed to find no fault with the presentation and asked no questions. However, intermittently during his responses to questions she turned to the students near her and spoke to them in fluent Chinese. The students' reactions changed rapidly from uncomfortable silences to animated argument, thoughtfulness and even friendly laughter.

Wang Qu Qing was in the group around her and, though he sometimes smiled at what she was saying, he also seemed to be arguing with her. Before Ian had finished his lecture Qu Qing had moved closer to where Ian was standing. As soon as the formal presentation was over he was speaking enthusiastically to the scientist, telling him about how he was planning to read everything he could find in the field of population control. Janet, overhearing him, believed him. He would learn this subject just as expeditiously as he had taught himself English and Russian.

Janet and Mary walked out together and Janet smiled and introduced herself. "I've seen you at the Friendship Hotel. In the Chinese dining room. How long have you been in China?" she asked. "You speak as if you were born here."

"As a matter of fact I was," Mary Allen laughed. "My parents were missionaries here before the liberation. I was born in Hunan Province and I spoke Chinese before I did English."

"Oh, how I envy you! It's so much easier to learn a language as a child. I have to struggle for every word I pick up."

"I know some excellent teachers of Chinese. If you're interested I'll put you in touch with one."

"Thanks, I *am* interested. But I won't be in Beijing long. I'm just visiting friends for a few days before I go north. But maybe Carol would like some tutoring." She said it as Carol came up behind them.

"I don't know," Carol said. "Not knowing Chinese seems an advantage in teaching English. I'm not always being tempted to translate for my students." Her normally friendly face had stiffened into hostility, and she made as if to move ahead of them.

"I always felt that way too," Janet said into the uncomfortable silence.

"It's a mystery to me how you can teach without knowing the language," Mary Allen said. "I'd never be able to do it."

"Why do you come here with your lies?" The low voice startled them. Most of the students, talking animatedly among themselves as they pressed toward the door, paid no attention to the English words. "You are not welcome here."

Mary Allen recovered and looked coolly and disdainfully at the young Chinese woman in the white lab coat who stared back at her, challenge in her stance and in the fixity of her eyes. Then they saw her face change from anger to something that looked almost like adoration, and followed her eyes. Ian Chen had noticed that something was happening and was making his way through the crowd toward them.

"You have no right to interfere with the great work he is doing," the Chinese woman said quickly, and turned and ducked through a door nearby.

When Ian came up to them Mary's voice was sarcastic. "Have you come to apologize for the bad manners of your little assistant?"

"No," he answered slowly. "I can imagine what she said to you but I won't apologize. She's not my little assistant. She's Dr. Hu Jiang, a famous geneticist here. And she has very strong opinions about our work."

"She's also very fond of you." Somehow she managed to make it sound like a dirty joke.

"As I am of her." He tossed it off lightly and changed the subject. "I'm looking forward to seeing Mark tomorrow."

She said nothing.

"I see you've met Carol—and Dr. Janet Eldine."

"I was just about to suggest that the three of us get to know each other a little better. I know a restaurant that serves a great tea. Come along, Carol. I'd like to know more about your system of teaching English without knowing Chinese."

"We'd better not have a really great tea," Janet said. "We've got a banquet this evening." But she wanted to take advantage of the opportunity to go off on impulse this way. Such opportunities were rare in a country where one did not speak the language.

Besides, the woman had charm and, Janet was sure, deliberate purposefulness in her presence here. She was curious to know more about what made Mary Allen tick. "Carol?"

Carol bit her lip, unwilling to be less tolerant of Mary Allen than Ian obviously was. "Okay," she said finally.

Janet explained briefly to Ching and Cai, and the three women waited for Mary's cab while the students piled back into the bus and returned to the college. Before they had left the room Ian was already bending over a microscope.

In the cab Carol held herself stiffly, unable to hide her dislike. It must be out of loyalty to Ian, Janet thought. She can't know all that much about Mary's work, or even care that much about the issues. Can it be that she's jealous of Mary's relationship with Ian?

And just what *was* that relationship? Mary certainly did nothing to temper her sarcasm and contempt when she talked to Ian, and he seemed placating—even loving. Very curious.

"I'm not going to pull any punches just because Ian and I are friends." Mary's words startled Janet, as if the woman had been reading her mind. "I think it's all wrong and I'll continue to say so even though I expect to be kicked out of the country any minute."

"Do you mean that?" Janet had stopped thinking of China as intolerant of dissent. The people she met, the friends she had made had such a wide variety of opinions about everything.

"Oh yes. I sometimes get the feeling that it's not so much that I disagree with the policy as that the Chinese are hurt and insulted that I don't love China unconditionally. They'll give lip service to the fact that 'Things are not easy here; there are many things we do not have.' But given that, everyone is expected to love everything else about the country."

Janet laughed.

"And it's because I *do* love the country and the people," Mary went on soberly, "that I'm so vehemently opposed to what they're doing."

"Do you think an outsider has the right to tell China what she should do?" Carol asked. "After all, you aren't Chinese."

"It's not only China I'm talking about, it's the world. Just because one country has a problem feeding its people, that doesn't mean the answer lies in abortion and sterilization and tampering with genes. It's a problem the world must solve. There's more than enough land on earth and there could be enough food. It's a question of development and distribution. But as long as we treat the matter of population as an individual national problem we'll try to solve it only by devaluing life."

"Then it's not only birth control you're concerned with; it's the business of improving the quality of life on a global level."

"Exactly. It often comes out like merely an antiabortion position, but that's not what I'm trying to do at all. Unfortunately my editor's policy doesn't leave me much room to deal with the broader solutions. But at least I get them in sometimes. It's more of a chance than any other paper is willing to give me."

Janet was skeptical, though she couldn't be absolutely sure that she was remembering accurately. But she could recall no connection between Mary Allen and concern with anything besides a virulent antiabortion stance.

"How well do you know Dr. Chen?" Carol asked abruptly. "Or are you just his enemy?"

Mary evaded the questions though a small frown appeared above the bridge of her nose. "He's a remarkable man, isn't he?"

Janet could feel the tension between them. Mary sat back, a pleasant smile on her lips. Carol wasn't smiling. Janet had never seen her look so grim.

"We *are* friends, you know, and I respect him. He's a man of great integrity. And we've agreed to disagree." Mary smiled again as if she was appealing to Carol to be her friend too. "Ian wants me to raise questions about his work."

After tea Janet asked the cab driver to let her out at the gate to the Friendship Hotel compound so she could walk to her building, while the others rode on to their rooms. She was beginning to feel the lack of exercise since coming to China. Her days were so filled and her hosts so generous with chauffeur-driven cars and taxis that she was not walking as much as she was accustomed to at home. She had a horror of seeing the pounds add up on her small figure, and she had been reminded of the danger in the company of Mary and Carol, both of them tall and beautifully thin. They probably wore the same size clothes; even their shoes might fit each other. They both had very small feet for such tall women—as small as Janet's. But, she thought, it didn't look as if there would ever be any friendly borrowing between them.

As she got out of the cab she was nearly run down by that fool of an Algerian on his motorbike. She tried to feel some sympathy for the man but he was such a pig. Shattering the peace of the compound at all hours of the day and night on that awful machine. With his once white, old-fashioned car coat flapping out behind him like a dirty flag of defiance. She wondered how long it would be before the authorities intervened to stop him.

The first time she had spoken to him had been in the dining room while they both waited for service from the woman at the counter. If one wanted beer or a small side dish of bean curd or a slice of cake for dessert one had to pick it up at the counter. Main dishes were ordered from the waitress who came to the table.

Standing and waiting to pay for her dessert, she made a casual comment to the man standing beside her and he had grunted a reply. When she went back to her table he followed her. For a while he sat and ate and said nothing to her. Finally she was moved to make desperate small talk because his sitting there silently seemed so peculiar. "I notice your accent is French," she observed pleasantly. He said nothing for a while. Then: "I am not French," he denied with such glowering intensity that she felt she had insulted him. "I have no country. I am bereft of my country."

She was startled into silence, scrabbling through her memory for some situation in recent history that might explain what he had said. Palestinian? That didn't square with the French accent. One of the minority group in Sri Lanka? India? South Africa? None of these fitted either his physical appearance or his accent.

"Algeria was my country." His great anger was apparent in the way he bit off and spat out each word. "Algeria was my country until we were betrayed."

"B-betrayed?"

"The French! They turned the country over to the rabble! *We* made the country prosperous. *We* did the important work! Now we are dispossessed and my Algeria will be destroyed."

"They made you leave Algeria?"

He looked at her, his face contorted with fury. "They did not make me leave! I could not remain and see the country run by *them*. There was no place there for *us*."

From what she remembered of the situation in Algeria, she thought he must be talking about De Gaulle's agreement to Algerian independence. That was in 1962, and all three million of the French population had gone to France, leaving the seven million Moslems with the country to themselves. This man was about thirty-five years old, she estimated. Which meant that all this had happened when he was a teenager. A long time for hatred to fester while he roamed the world feeling like an outsider everywhere.

"Wh-what do you do here in China?" she asked, trying to move away from his anger and obsession. She was almost afraid of him. He seemed not so much out of control as not *modulated*. He didn't respond in a social situation the way most people did.

She saw the anger recede slightly; his eyes didn't look quite so crazy. "I translate for the Xinhua, the Chinese news service. They print a small French publication—mostly for tourists."

"Oh, that sounds interesting. Where do they distribute it?"

"Do you speak French?" he asked abruptly.

"Very badly, I'm afraid."

"Americans!" He dismissed Americans.

Her eyebrows went up. "You don't think much of Americans?"

"I have met some of you."

She didn't like being lumped like that into a group for purposes of rejection. Before she could tell him where to get off, he said, "Do you know the American, Mary Allen?"

"The writer? I know her writing."

"What right does she have to come here and say what China should do? She is not Chinese! Just like the French! They come to my country and say what we should do. They take the country from us and give it to *them!*"

"Well," Janet tried to lighten it up, "she can hardly do much to change the government of China. She's only one person with a point of view."

"Did you know her mother was French?" he asked, his anger building again.

"N-no. I really don't know anything about her."

"I know her well! She thinks she knows what is best for China. They should chase her from here. As we should have chased the French! But we were betrayed."

Janet breathed a sigh of relief when he gulped the last of his tea and dashed out of the dining room. Without even a word of parting. Whew! she thought. A very disturbing man.

Now she suddenly remembered having seen him with Mary Allen; they had been eating together.

The great tea did nothing to spoil Janet's appetite for the great banquet that evening. When the toasts had been made—to the foreign experts who came to help China and were "warmly welcome," to the "continued friendship of our two countries," to the success of Dr. Chen's experiments—the almost ritual service of the food began. There were all the special dishes reserved for festive occasions: *dzaodzi*, those tiny pockets of dough with a savory pork filling; lotus hearts sautéed in a feather-light batter; strips of deliciously spiced pork and shrimp puffs that were eaten the way Americans eat potato chips. And, of course, roast duck. Even Carol, obviously aware every minute of Ian sitting beside her, ate with pleasure. He did too.

She had suppressed a smile when she saw Ian skillfully maneuver Carol to the seat on his right at the round table in the private dining room of the restaurant. And they had almost finished the meal when she heard him say, "I'll drive you home." Carol nodded.

The final toast was to their meeting again, preferably at such a munificent table. To the Chinese, good food was an essential element of the ritual of life. They appreciated it and made it a part of their important times. That was fine with Janet. She was no slouch herself when it came to eating good food, and Chinese food certainly qualified. She felt sleek, sated and well cared for when they all rose from the table. Their hosts saw Carol and Ian into his car and waved them off, smiling and bowing. The banquet for the foreign experts had gone well.

Five

JANET WENT TO CAROL'S ROOMS the next morning to tell her that she would share her ride to Beijing Xue Yuan. Janet and her old friend Mrs. Hua had an appointment to discuss the problems of the English Department in the new university at Huhehot. Dorothy came in right behind her. Carol was getting into a flowered cotton skirt that was guaranteed to make her students gasp in disbelief. Dorothy whistled and Carol just smiled.

"I hear you left the banquet with the gorgeous Ian Chen," Dorothy said.

"What? How did you know that? Oh." She looked at Janet.

"Not me," Janet said. "I haven't seen her since the banquet."

"Don't you know yet that there are no secrets in China? There are certainly none at the Friendship Hotel."

"Okay," Carol said. "Yes, I had a great time. No, I don't want to talk about it. Yes, I'll probably see him again. No, I don't have time to say another word now; I've got to get ready for work." A horn beeped briefly outside. "And there's my ride."

"Then I won't tell you my news."

"Tell me while I finish dressing." And she walked into the bedroom to stand in front of the half-length mirror mounted on the old-fashioned chifferobe door.

Dorothy followed her in and made herself comfortable on the unused bed. She never batted an eye, though she knew very well that the floor maids had not yet had time to make up the beds. Janet leaned against the door frame.

"Well, John Peter will be here today."

Carol smiled serenely into the mirror. "From where?"

"From Tokyo. John Peter Philip Brigham."

"Oh. Japanese."

"No, you fool! English! He's been teaching in Tokyo and this is his school break. He's going to stay with me." Dorothy lived in the building next door, a hotel mainly for transients that was part of the Friendship Hotel complex of hotels, apartment houses, restaurants and shops.

"Won't that create difficulties?"

"Nope, it's all fixed up with the maids. Two boxes of chocolates and a word about my 'cousin.' They live in such close quarters here, it would never occur to them to question my giving room to my cousin."

"They may not care what the foreigners do, but they are certainly not stupid," Janet said.

Dorothy shrugged. "At any rate, he'll be here for a whole week. Isn't that lovely?"

"Lovely," Carol agreed. "When will he get here?"

"This afternoon. The unit will let me have a driver to pick him up."

"That's very generous, isn't it? I'll never get over how nice they are to us foreigners."

Dorothy grinned. "You're developing quite an affection for the Chinese, aren't you?"

Carol grinned back and said nothing except, "Goodbye, Dorothy. We'll leave you to find your own way out."

As Janet and Carol closed the door behind them, they heard her chuckle. They ran down the steps to the waiting car.

For a while Janet watched Carol teach her class. Half her mind seemed to be in a sort of rosy haze while the other half functioned on automatic. She smiled at and complimented the students as they struggled with English. She held up pictures and asked them to identify the objects pictured. She had them follow directions and then let them give directions to one another. And every once in a while she favored them all with a smile so inappropriately dazzling that they stared at her speechless. Janet would have bet that when the morning was over she would hardly remember what she had been doing.

Janet wandered out of the room. She still had some time before she was to meet Mrs. Hua and she wanted a few minutes to enjoy the perfect fall day. Infants and grandmothers strolled the campus before lunch. Students walked with their empty bowls toward their own dining room. They would not eat there because no seats were provided. Most of them would take their filled bowls back to their rooms and eat in the company of the five or six roommates crowded into a space the size of her kitchen at home. She often wondered how they managed to look so bright and clean and even-tempered, living in such cramped quarters with so few comforts. And they were all so grateful for the opportunity to be here, to be studying. She admired their enthusiasm and their fortitude.

She mused on the romance apparently developing between Ian Chen and Carol. They made a lovely couple—both so beautiful to look at. And then she remembered the look on Carol's face when Mary had talked about Ian. Was there going to be trouble at the Friendship Hotel?

Not that there wasn't always something stirring in the pot of the foreign compound. It was like a small town that was serene and peaceful only on the surface. At the moment the compound was gossiping about one of the foreign experts from Oregon who had been having a torrid romance with another from Argentina. It was a mystery how she had found out about it, but suddenly the Argentinian's wife had turned up. And now all the public displays of affection were lavished on the wife, while the abandoned lover sat hot-eyed and watched them—from a distant table in the dining room, from the other side of the swimming pool, from several tiers above in the auditorium where films were shown every week. People observed it all and discussed it *ad nauseam.* There wasn't much more to distract them here in this isolated enclave than there would be in any other affluent middle-class ghetto in the States.

She saw Mrs. Hua come to the door of the classroom building and her thoughts switched immediately to the job she had to do in Huhehot. The difficulty with setting up a new English Department was in getting teachers to staff it. There was no shortage of English-speaking foreigners eager to leave home for an adventurous year in China, but staff members who left after a year gave no stability or continuity to any teaching program. Chinese speakers of unaccented English were rare, most of them already holding responsible jobs.

Maybe Mrs. Hua, who chaired the English Department here, would have some ideas for her. "Ah, Dr. Aldane. You are here!" Even she couldn't pronounce Janet's name. "Let us go to my office where we will be comfortable."

Janet smiled with pleasure at the unfailing courtesy. She hoped that the people in Huhehot, where foreigners were not so common, would welcome her as kindly.

The hour went quickly and she took her leave when it was time for lunch. Meals were still awkward, even though they were friends. She would not be invited to the Chinese faculty dining room, and eating in the Foreign Students Building required advance notice to the cook and the acquisition of food tickets. And, in the end, a Chinese person was still reluctant to eat in public with a foreigner. She walked to the taxi office to wait for a ride back to the Friendship Hotel. When she got there Dorothy and John Peter were in the Western dining room.

"Janet, come and sit with us," Dorothy called when Janet came in.

"What are you doing home at this time of day?" Janet asked.

"Oh, this is John's first day here and I just couldn't waste it at work!"

John sat stolidly. He appeared able to absorb all of Dorothy's effervescence without even burping. A calm and contented man.

"I hope you enjoy your stay," Janet told him.

"I'm sure I will." He obviously meant that—and didn't think it necessary to say anything more.

Dorothy smiled at him fondly and then settled in for a pleasant gossip. "Carol is smitten, isn't she? What's he really like?"

"Ian Chen? Well, that first impression was right, I think. He's a fascinating man."

She arched an eyebrow.

Janet frowned a little. Dorothy liked playing the empty-headed hedonist and it sometimes bothered Janet, who knew she was intelligent and astute. Her course in Western literature that she taught at Beijing University had established her reputation for knowledgeability and sensitivity and Janet had been impressed early in their friendship with how well informed she was about world politics. This time she refused to play straight man to her foolishness and she answered seriously. "Unlike some scientists I've known, he's amazingly concerned about what might happen as a result of his work. Do you know, Mary Allen said he actually encourages her to attack what he does?"

"What on earth for? Does he have some kind of death wish?"

"No-o-o. If she's telling the truth, I think he just wants to create discussion about the whole business of population control. There's something about it that disturbs him."

"You mean he doesn't really believe in it?"

"I don't know. But I get the feeling that intellectually the idea of forced control is distasteful to him." She shook her head. "I'll have to know more about him. We're all having dinner tonight."

"All?"

"Mary and her husband, Carol and Ian. They've asked me too."

Mary had invited Ian, Carol and Janet to have dinner with her and her husband, who was visiting Beijing. Janet had demurred at first, unwilling to make a fifth in the group, but Mary had insisted and Carol had joined her in urging Janet to come along.

"Oh, good. I'd like to know more about him myself—from an objective observer, that is."

"Yes." Janet sat there bemused. She was sorry that Jiao Zhong En was not in Beijing. He would have added something special to the conversation and she knew she would have had no trouble convincing him to join them. Since meeting Janet on her last stay in China he had very quickly begun to ignore all the usual strictures surrounding association with foreigners.* Finally she said, "I think Mary Allen is trying to seduce Carol."

"What?"

* *Murder in China.*

"Oh, don't be silly. I mean seduce intellectually. Maybe emotionally too. She's making a strong bid to be Carol's friend."

"You think Carol would support Mary against Ian Chen?"

"M-m-m. It's not that simple. Even Ian supports Mary against Ian Chen."

Dorothy was understandably confused but she didn't pursue it. She looked at John, who hadn't said a word for most of lunch, and moved her chair closer so she could rub shoulders with him. "Let's talk again about all this. It sounds very interesting. Maybe after you've had dinner."

After that the conversation made room for John, who talked amusingly about life in Tokyo, which was more and more reminding him of life in London or New York. "Very often," he said, "I drive out to the country just to remind myself that I'm living in an ancient, exotic culture completely different than my own. I keep worrying that the next time I drive out I'll be in Surrey or Brighton and that I won't have left England at all."

"How long have you lived in Japan?" Janet asked.

"Five years. I feel very much at home there, you know."

"Your friends—are they all Japanese?" She was thinking of her own life in China three years before. She had somehow managed to avoid the society of foreigners in Beijing. Most of the friends she had made were Chinese.

"Oh no," he said. "About half and half. Many English-speaking foreigners somehow gravitate toward each other there."

It was only when Janet left them at the door of Dorothy's hotel and had gone to her own rooms that she wondered if Dorothy's friend had ever met Mary Allen's husband Mark in Tokyo.

Six

JANET OPENED TO THE KNOCK. Carol and Ian stood there, arms linked. "Ready?" he asked.

They ran down the steps of the hotel and out to the car. The Chinese chauffeur nodded to them and turned on the ignition. Ian must be very important indeed to have a car at his disposal even in the evening for a private social occasion, Janet thought.

"I'm looking forward to meeting Mary's husband. It should be an interesting evening."

Had Carol managed to overcome her initial feelings of anger and hostility toward Mary or was she just trying to suppress them? "Have you met him?" Janet asked Ian.

"Yes. We've all known each other for years. I met him about the same time I met Mary. Back home. She was in a crowd of reporters interviewing me after our first breakthrough on a male contraceptive. I took her to lunch and Mark met us at the restaurant."

"You really are friends, aren't you? Anyone reading her articles would assume you were deadly enemies."

"No, you'll see—and hear—for yourself. I like Mary very much. I respect her. I think she feels the same about me."

Mary and Mark came out of the building next door and joined them. The couple had a favorite restaurant in a small side street off Wangfujing. The short drive gave all of them the time they needed to be sure that they liked each other enough to have a very pleasant evening together.

They talked about life in China and Mark was able to contrast it to his experiences in Japan, where he was a banker and manufacturers' representative. Janet wondered why he didn't try to put his skills to work in China and so be closer to Mary. But they seemed happy with each other. If there had ever been conflict between them over their separate careers it was not apparent now.

"Why do you think the Japanese are not as seriously into population control as the Chinese are?" Janet asked Mark. "They've got so much less space, they're so crowded, one would think they'd be more concerned about it."

"The Japanese are concerned," he answered. "They just can't drag themselves away from their expanding economy to concentrate on their expanding population. Though abortion is very common—almost routine. Maybe they think the problem will work itself out." He spoke lightly. Apparently the matter didn't absorb him as much as it did his wife.

"Maybe they know," Mary retorted, "that the problem will never be solved by birth control but by the redistribution of people and food."

"Maybe what they're counting on is the kind of redistribution they've tried before. How many times in their modern history have they tried to move into other countries?"

"No, Carol," Mark replied. "I think they're finished with that kind of expansion. They're much better at manufacturing than they are at conquering."

"Do you think the countries of the world will ever be able to cooperate enough to work on an international plan for sharing land and food?" Janet asked. "You know, the United States has so much surplus food that the government buys to maintain farm prices. But it rots in warehouses while local and state governments argue about who should pay for getting it to the people who need it."

"They'll have to! How much longer do you think we can stand by and watch people starving in Africa or dying in the streets of Bangladesh?" It had taken only a few words for Mary to change from relaxed social hostess to intense protagonist in her cause. Both Janet and Carol were interested in her point of view and their questions fired her zeal. She seemed to forget that one of her guests was deeply involved in research that sought to accomplish exactly what she was condemning.

Janet's eyes slid obliquely to Ian's face. He sat expressionless, listening to the well-reasoned arguments that virtually relegated population control to the same categories as suicide, murder and war, and seemed to examine them thoroughly from all sides for flaws, for gaps. How could he sit so calmly and hear her equate his work with the destruction of human life? Occasionally he asked a question or offered some factual information that Mary seemed to have overlooked but he never defended what he did or presented counterarguments. He actually appeared to encourage her, helped her strengthen her point of view. Only once Janet thought she saw a look of pain flash across his face but it was gone so quickly she decided she must have imagined it.

"I remember that Mao Zedong was once opposed to birth control," Janet laughed. "The Chinese have a tendency to behave as if the last policy is the only one they ever heard of. Publicly, at least."

"Is that true?" asked Carol. "I thought the Communist regime decreed almost at once that population control was necessary if China was to emerge as a strong nation."

"It's true. Even though the country has always lived with the threat of famine and flood, Mao thought that birth control was a capitalist idea that was systematically spread by Westerners to keep China weak," Janet said.

"Don't you see?" demanded Mary. "Being against birth control is still in the memory of people living today. I'll bet most of them are against it, and they won't need much encouragement to resist the government and reject the policy."

"It's a pipe dream! How can your articles in the U.S. get to all the people in China?"

"Really, Mark, that's not very sophisticated of you. Getting to the peasants and workers is hardly necessary. All I have to do is influence a few key people to take the initiative here."

"They'll get you out of China long before you're able to manage that."

"It doesn't matter." Mary was adamant. "I don't have to be here. They get the American publications and I know they read them. At least the top educators and scientists do. That's all that's needed."

Janet laughed to break the tension that threatened to become anger. "Who knows?" she said. "Revolutions have started with less ammunition and very few people convinced of the need for rebellion. I doubt that the American revolutionaries could have mustered a majority for their side."

"Until the war had been won, that is," Carol chimed in.

At some point in the discussion Mary began to speak to Carol as if they were allies. Carol was a writer herself. Her popular articles on education were widely read in the United States. Mary seemed to take it for granted that Carol would use her writing skills and contacts with the journals to spread the word. Was she assuming that Carol's interest and her questions meant that she was ready to join forces with her?

"We'll collaborate on a series of articles in a magazine like *Omni* or *Scientific American*. They'll accept articles with your name on them."

Carol smiled uncertainly. "You want to collaborate with me. That's very flattering . . ."

"The articles can be in the form of a dialogue between us—so all the questions can be answered. It's a great idea!" Mary was carried away with enthusiasm and moving Carol along with her.

Janet's eyebrows went up. Dialogue, my foot. She was saying that Carol's article would be an interview with her, so *she* could answer all the questions.

"You're a writer too, Janet. You can write about this. Let everyone know what the facts are."

Instinctively she had hit on Janet's approach to controversial issues. Janet wanted people to know all sides so they could make educated decisions. And she had long thought that the strident shouting on both sides of the abortion issue was just that—emotional yelling into the political maelstrom to get a decision here and there, a political reversal here and there. What was needed was a clear examination of population problems from the perspective of world needs and worldwide resources for meeting those needs. What Ian said he wanted, and what Mary Allen said too—but wasn't doing.

But she never responded well to pressure. "It needs discussing, certainly." She smiled. "But not by me at this time." Her voice was pleasant but unmistakably firm.

"Ah, a true academic. You people don't often take vocal sides on really big controversies, do you? But then, that's a reason for teaching, isn't it? So safe."

The attack had a barely disguised viciousness that seemed to fit Mary's personality more consistently than the smiling friendliness she assumed. The way she was pushing Carol to work with her; the way she overrode Mark's comments; the amiable possessiveness with which she invested everything she said to Ian—Mary would not easily accept frustration of her wishes.

"Do you know that last year there was about one abortion for every three births in Japan?" Mark asked his wife. "You don't think anything should be done to prevent that kind of whole-sale—"

"That's not the point. Abortion and contraception are equally bad."

"Really! Well, since you've never had to be bothered with either one, you're the ideal expert, aren't you? What about the natural need for sex? Do you expect people to forget about it until your 'distribution' system is ready?"

Mary's lips tightened.

"Sorry," Mark said blandly. "Shouldn't have mentioned sex."

Mary's mouth twisted on the word, as if no gentleman would ever mention it. How in the world could she be so involved with birth control and still be a prude about discussing sex?

"Enough about work," Ian said heartily. "Mark, just before I came here, there was a lot of talk in the U.S. about bringing over Japan's management methods to increase production. Just what is there about Japanese management that makes it so successful?"

Mark turned eagerly to answer Ian's question. But Mary interrupted. "Ian, *you* know where I'm coming from, don't you? *You* know how important my work is?"

"Yes, *your* work!" Mark burst in. "It's always *your* work. And while you're at it, you'll ruin Ian. You pretend to be his friend, but you go right on trying to destroy him."

"No, Mark. You don't understand. There are plenty of us publishing our side of the story. I want Mary's side presented too—as accurately and forcefully as she knows how. That's the only way to get the right decisions made."

"How can such a brainy man be so gullible?" There was desperation in Mark's voice, and for a moment Janet thought he would burst into tears.

Into the silence that had fallen at the table, Ian said, "Look, if we're finished eating, let's go." And he herded them all out of the restaurant. "The rest of the evening is on me."

He led them through a maze of narrow side streets over to Sun Yatsen Road and a modest building whose doors were thrown open to receive the lines of people. He produced tickets at the door and they found seats in the dimly lit auditorium. In a very few minutes every single seat was taken by smiling, chattering people.

"What is it?" Janet asked, excited as the prospect of any form of theater always made her.

"Not Peking Opera," Mark groaned.

"Oh, don't you like it? I love it—the colors of the satins and brocades, the pageantry and stylized movements! I can watch it for hours!"

"That's it. It goes on for hours!" He groaned again.

"No, it isn't Peking Opera," Ian laughed. "I wouldn't do that to you, Mark. It's a new play, written by a friend of mine. We'll meet him after the final curtain and you can tell him what you think of it."

"You'll have to translate for me," Janet said.

"Okay, you'll get a running translation—every word."

She made a face, having experienced Chinese theater before this, where the audience talked incessantly throughout the performance. No one would mind another running commentary. Surprisingly, it was only at the movies that Chinese audiences were silent. Maybe the new technology brought forth new behaviors.

Traditional entertainments were accompanied by traditional modes of response. She wondered how everybody managed to hear so much of the dialogue.

Ian translated for her and Carol. Though Mark leaned away from Mary and also tried to hear what Ian was saying, it was clear from an occasional comment that he understood Chinese.

The play had much of the stylized movement of the ancient opera and it was set in the past, but it was a modern play posing a contemporary dilemma. It had a hero who agonized over the severity of punishment meted out to those who interfered with the modernization of the country. Was it possible, he asked, for the country to achieve its goals while still permitting some individuals to cling to the old ways? Or must all opposition to progress be ruthlessly suppressed? Boldly—because in this society the arts still were expected to provide solutions to social problems—the playwright ended the play with the question unanswered.

After the show they went backstage and were photographed with the cast still dressed in their colorful costumes. They were also introduced to the playwright, who seemed pathetically eager to hear their opinions of his work and very grateful when the observations were positive. Later Ian dropped Mary and Mark off at their building and Janet got out in front of her hotel. As if by prearrangement Carol remained in the car when he drove across the compound to his apartment.

Carol woke Janet at six the next morning. "I must talk to you," she said.

"Ah well," Janet sighed with exaggerated resignation. "When in China . . ." The joke died on her lips. Carol looked haggard, almost ugly. The gray blouse and red scarf she wore emphasized the greenish pallor of her face and leached the color from her bright red hair. Janet looked compassionately at the drained face, thinking she must be tortured about something to have her beauty almost extinguished. "Come on in. Would you like a cup of tea?" She picked up the thermos of hot water left at her door by the maid and put tea bags to steep. She ran a comb through her hair and they settled themselves comfortably in the easy chairs in the living room.

"I'm thinking seriously of working with Mary—writing up the whole issue for the popular science media."

Janet nodded. "I think Ian wants you two to be friends."

"Yes." She looked grim. "But I'm not doing it because Ian wants me to. I'll make up my own mind!"

Who's arguing? Janet thought. But she said nothing.

"Do you think it would be disloyal of me to collaborate with her?"

"Disloyal?" Janet didn't ask the next question, but it was clear. Had the relationship between Carol and Ian progressed so far that a total loyalty was to be expected?

"I—I feel as if I've known him for years," Carol said shyly. Slowly the flush deepened on her fair skin.

So, Janet thought. She's been to bed with him already. Things were a lot simpler before women recognized that they also had *minds* to reconcile with physical attraction. Now what?

"It's not that I think I ought to agree with him on everything," Carol said almost defensively. "I'm my own person, you know. And I intend to keep control over my life."

Too much protest, Janet thought. Poor woman, she's afraid of him. His strength, his power.

"He's a very strong man." Carol seemed to be reading her mind —or Janet was reading *hers.*

And then the words were spilling out of Carol. Too much to keep inside—too much beauty, too much conflict, too much fear:

When they had gone to his apartment last night he had asked her, "How does scrambled eggs sound to you?"

"Like ambrosia."

The meal they prepared together was a delicious mélange of East and West, both of them jostling each other in the small kitchen, teasing when a spoon was dropped. ("No expert drops his tools," she chided him.) Indignantly rejecting advice. ("Soy sauce and ginger are just what eggs have always needed!" he pronounced.) Knowing that the joking and busyness only thinly masked the tension between them.

"Mary Allen is a very interesting woman," she said casually.

"One of the loves of my life," he answered lightly. "An independent, rational human being who can also be loving and nurturing."

Hmph, Janet thought. Something missing in the nurturing of her husband. Aloud she said, "He feels like that about her when what comes out in her writing is a simple antiabortion stance? The humanitarian ideas never get printed. Do you want to be identified with that point of view?"

"No, I don't. But . . . but . . ." Her voice trailed away.

What confusion! Did Carol want to identify with Mary and so get the kind of admiration from Ian that Mary got? Was she just proclaiming her independence from any man by taking a stand—no matter how wobbly—against Ian's work? Never had Janet seen a more striking example of intellect weakened by neurotic emotions.

Yet Carol was able—acutely observant as she could be—to understand the cause of the attachment between Mary and Ian. "I think," she told him, "that Mary speaks to your own self-doubt. You encourage her because she puts words to some of the thoughts you want to talk about."

He admitted it and admired her perceptiveness. And she admired him for appreciating her mind.

"Set the table—fast," he ordered. "Before this masterpiece gets cold."

She set the small table with a length of ivory and gold brocade he pulled from a drawer. "Picked it up for a cousin. I'll get something else for her." The rose-pattern dishes looked like antique china, and her heart nearly stopped at his casual handling of them. She looked skeptically at the exquisite cloisonné and ivory chopsticks, hoping she would be able to manage them for scrambled eggs. They poured Tsingtao beer into delicately fluted glasses, also probably bought for someone back home. It was a table as exotic as the gingered eggs, as intriguingly different as Ian's deep-set eyes, as memorable as everything that had happened to her since she had fallen in front of his car.

It frightened her to think how chancy life was, what the odds were against their ever having met in this very large world. She pretended to brush against him accidentally, just to feel the reality of him for an instant, to reassure herself that this was not all a dream.

They ate by the light of a single guttering candle. The jokes became fewer, the silences longer as they neared the end of the meal.

When she had opened her eyes this morning, Ian lay fast asleep, his face turned toward her. The memory of their lovemaking first made her smile dreamily and stretch and purr like a cat. It had been every woman's fantasy of love—gentle, strong, completely fulfilling. He had used her body like a virtuoso, as a master uses the priceless violin he owns. Suddenly she felt wide awake, frightened.

Frowning, she sat up, wondering what was wrong. That was it: he had used her as if he owned her. Masterfully, yes. But like an instrument, passive, responsive to his touch, to his skill, but without initiative, without will of her own. He hadn't given her a chance to participate actively in making love, as she did naturally. He was the one who had done all the loving; she had just received him, like a placid . . .

She took a deep, sobbing breath, trying to stop the buildup of fury her thoughts were causing. Methodically, bringing what logic she could to the process, she sat there trying to understand what had happened between them. This was not how they had made love the first night. Then they had been equals, two strong people seeking no commitment, no promises, above all not subjugation. She thought that was what they both wanted, but apparently she had been mistaken.

It served her right, taking up with a stranger! She knew nothing about this man, but he had tricked her into abandoning her usual caution. And now she was learning about him. He wanted a lover, but one he could manage, manipulate. Own. A cook and a concubine—that was what he wanted to make of her! Well, he had the wrong woman! She'd be damned if she would take on that role.

She slammed out of the bed, wrapping the brocade quilt around herself.

"Wh-what . . . Hey, bring back that cover!" He rolled over, startled. His tousled sleepiness touched some spot of tenderness in her, but she shut it off from consciousness and stood there, five feet from the bed, glaring at him. The look finally penetrated. He sat up, propping the pillow against the headboard behind him. "Something wrong?" he asked mildly.

Too nonchalant, she thought. He knows exactly what he did! He started to get out of bed. "No!" she almost shouted. "Just stay where you are!"

"Carol, what's the matter?"

"I said stay away! Don't touch me! You tricked me!" The sound of her own voice was increasing her agitation and she made an enormous effort to regain control. Finally she was able to say quietly, "I'm going to get dressed and leave. I can't talk about it now. I'll be out of here in ten minutes." And she scooped up her things as she ran from the bedroom to the living room to the bathroom. Ian had the grace to say nothing, and when she came out of the bathroom he was dressed too.

"We'll talk about this later," he said.

When she started to protest, he insisted, "We *will* talk about this, Carol. I'll see you tonight."

She closed the door behind her and walked briskly to her own door, her heels echoing on the path. It was still dark. There wasn't a soul around, not even the soldiers guarding the compound were anywhere in evidence. Thank heaven it was Saturday and she didn't have to go to work; her students had been given the day to study.

"Do you know, he *wanted* me to work with Mary—to help her attack his work! He manipulated me into that. I *hate* being manipulated—used."

For more than an hour she seesawed back and forth between certainty, the confidence that she had made the right decisions, and frightening doubt, the equal certainty that her decisions were mistakes she would regret for the rest of her life. She punctuated her indecision with furious attacks on Ian: "It was *his* idea to get me involved in this! *His* decision that I collaborate with Mary! He's using me!"

"If you think that, Carol, then do what you want to do. You would have met Mary sooner or later because she's Ian's friend. How your relationship with her develops is up to you."

"He says he's very fond of her. Do you think they were lovers?"

Janet couldn't bring herself to answer. This required more than a few casual words of comfort from a friend. Carol needed a lot more help than that.

Seven

WHEN JANET CAME OUT into the corridor she thought something might be up. The klatsch of talking maids didn't usually get started until late afternoon. Mornings were spent busily working —changing bed linens, sweeping the carpets, emptying wastepaper baskets and distributing jugs of boiled water. A little later the bathrooms in the suites were scrubbed and the furniture dusted. Occasionally a homemade mousetrap was built—a flat of cardboard smeared with some sticky substance surrounding a bit of food supposedly tempting to a mouse. More than once they had proudly displayed a captive rodent on the goo. She thought she would rather live with mice than with that disgusting mess under her bed. She wouldn't have been surprised to learn that the contraption attracted mice from wherever they roamed in the environment.

Now, only a little after eight o'clock in the morning, the women were already gathered at one end of the corridor talking excitedly. When she called good morning on her way out, one of them stopped her and tried to tell her what had happened.

"Foreign woman dead," she announced. Her eyes were round and her expression serious, but the announcement seemed to be made with relish. Like people everywhere privy to news of catastrophe in which they were not immediately involved.

Janet stopped with one foot on the stair. "Who?" she asked. "Where?"

The maid pointed to her left, through the wall. The other hotel, the one catering to foreigners who were staying in China for short periods of time. In her building the residents lived for a year or more, working on contracts with the various ministries. The only people she knew who lived next door were Dorothy and Mary Allen. Dorothy had been put there when she came because there had been no vacancies in Janet's building, and then she had just stayed on. She felt a clutch at her insides. Nonsense! There were a couple of hundred foreigners in that building!

"Do you know the foreign woman's name?" she asked.

The maid shook her head and turned back to the others. Her English was limited and she avoided extended conversations in a language she could hardly understand.

Outside Janet saw a khaki jeep parked near the hotel next door. The enormous red star on the side identified it as belonging to the People's Liberation Army, of which the security police were a branch. Stationed at the door of the hotel was a young soldier in the usual ill-fitting khaki, sternly turning the residents back as they came to the door on their way out to sightsee. She thought she recognized him, but it was difficult to tell. So many of the soldiers were young peasants with round faces and rosy cheeks, all with the same stern look they tried—against their natures—to assume, as if to assert the authority of their role and the seriousness of their business. The awful wrinkled uniforms completed the anonymity, and she couldn't say if this was one of the young men she had seen at the college where Mrs. Li had been murdered three years ago.

Looking up at him, she was undecided if she should go up the steps and ask for the man in charge. Perhaps he was the same one who had been in charge of the other case. She had never learned his name.

Why was she assuming this was also a murder case? If someone had died, the odds were that it was of natural causes. How many murders could occur in one's own vicinity in the course of a lifetime? Especially in a vicinity characterized by middle-class safeguards and cosseting?

At that moment the tall, good-looking officer she remembered came to the door to say something to the soldier. Before he turned back, he saw her and smiled in recognition. She was encouraged to walk up to him.

"Hello!" She put out her hand and he took it.

"We meet again," he noted. His excellent English included many of the clichés and anachronisms. He had learned the language mostly from outdated grammar books. But she knew that he was a reader. The anachronisms would soon disappear.

"What's happened?"

"One of your countrywomen," he told her, suppressing a smile at her un-Chinese directness.

"Murdered?" she demanded abruptly. She felt frightened; it made her manner even more brusque than usual.

He nodded.

"Who is it?" She got the words out with an effort, though no one would be able to detect what that effort cost her.

"A Mrs. Mary Allen."

He caught her arm as her eyes closed and she swayed. She clutched his other arm. She wasn't faint, only shocked. She clutched him because murder drained solidity from the world, made it soft, like gelatin.

In a moment she was able to open her eyes and begin her questions in earnest. "Who did it?"

As soon as the words were out she realized the question was not appropriate. Who? was one of the last questions in a murder case.

"How did it happen?"

His eyes clouded as if at an unpleasant memory. "With a knife," he said matter-of-factly. "You knew her?"

So much, she was able to observe, for the belief of most foreigners in China that the security police were aware of every move they made. Even here in the foreign compound there was more privacy than they imagined.

"Yes, I knew her. She spoke Chinese fluently."

The non sequitur surprised neither one of them. Knowing how to speak Chinese colored every aspect of the foreigner's life in China. And significantly affected the lives of those Chinese people who had any dealings with foreigners.

"We know of Mrs. Allen. She is a very famous writer."

"Of course. You would know her. The government hasn't been happy about her activities."

"They think she was no friend to China."

She nodded, understanding him. He had managed before to make it clear to her that he was not always in agreement with the practical policies of the government. Like most educated people, his points of view were arrived at independently. Rare in a soldier in any country.

"Perhaps you also know the woman who found her." He stepped aside for her to come into the lobby.

"Carol!" She moved impulsively toward her friend.

Carol sat in one of the easy chairs, her red hair hiding the hands she held to her face. Her head came up and Janet saw the remembered horror in her eyes. In a moment Carol was up and in her arms, crying in huge uncontrollable sobs. It was a long time before their intensity subsided a little and Janet could seat them both on the sofa. The officer stood in front of them waiting for the storm to be over.

Janet patted Carol soothingly. "What happened, Carol? Can you tell me?"

"Oh, Janet! It was horrible! Horrible! I can't believe it! I can't believe it!"

"What? What was it? What happened?"

Carol had knocked at the door of Mary's room at eight o'clock and waited impatiently. Her doubts were temporarily quiescent and she was eager to get on with the planning for her articles. She frowned and knocked again—a little harder this time. But there was still no answer from Mary.

Tentatively she turned the knob, not really expecting the door to be unlocked. But it was, and she opened it slowly, putting her head around the edge and calling out. "Mary, are you up? It's Carol. Your door's open, you know. Are you there?"

She stopped abruptly, half bent around the door, unable to take in what she was seeing. The room looked as if some crazy new-wave painter had thrown his bottle of poster paint at the walls. Enormous splashes of ocher had dried on the drab pale green with which all the hotel rooms were painted. Somewhere some of it must have spilled on the floor, because small, red-brown footprints marched across the worn carpet toward the door where she stood. They faded as they reached the door, as if the carpet had finally dried the shoe soles of the artist.

Straightening up and opening the door further, she damped down a small worm of horror and smiled uncertainly. "Hey, Mary," she called out. "What's been going on here? It looks like . . ."

The bed too was splotched with the ocher paint. Stained pillow half off the bed. Linens and brocade quilt ruined. Why did her feet refuse to move further into the room? Why was her heart suddenly hammering in her chest? She felt sick long before she saw anything that was sick-making.

Slowly her eyes moved around the room. The footprints led from the bathroom door on which a long smear of paint went from eye level down . . . Paint? . . . Her mouth felt dry and the worm of horror inside her wriggled and grew . . . and grew . . .

She didn't know she had been screaming until she became aware that she was surrounded by chattering Chinese women crowding through the door behind her, stopped where she was as if by an immovable barrier. The horror was outside her now and she saw it clearly.

Mary's hand reached through the half-open bathroom door, palm up, the fingers softly curled. It was covered with the reddish-brown paint. Dried blood. The realization snapped into her head and she suddenly knew why she was screaming.

By the time the security police got there she had been led down to the lobby by the crowd of hotel workers and was sitting with her head in her hands. She wanted desperately to go back to her own rooms but the women would not let her leave. Some in halting English, others in rapid Chinese urged her to stay until the police could talk to her. They brought her tea in a lidded cup and hovered over her like a flock of faded blue magpies with bright eyes and rosy cheeks, endlessly chattering.

She drank the tea gratefully, wishing they had sugared it, and she tried to block out the noise. Her only thoughts related to basic comforts—her own bed, sugar in her tea, peace and quiet. When the man's voice silenced the chattering, she breathed a sigh of relief.

"Mary! Murdered! Who could have done such a thing?" She began to sob again.

The officer motioned to his aide for a chair to be brought to him and he sat down facing the two women. When Carol's sobs had subsided again, he asked her, "What were you doing in Mrs. Allen's room?"

Carol lifted her head and looked at him as if she didn't quite understand what he was asking her. "I . . . I . . . uh . . . we . . . We had an appointment. We were meeting to discuss something. She told me to come at eight o'clock. Early, she said, because she had other things . . . other commitments . . . other people to talk to. . . ." Her voice faded away.

"How did you get into the room?"

"The door wasn't locked. I told you. I knocked, and when there was no answer, I tried the knob and the door opened. And then I saw . . . I saw . . . I saw . . ." Her breath came fast, as if she couldn't get enough air and her eyes mirrored the scene before her when she had opened the door.

"Do you know who might have done this thing?"

"No! I don't know! She was a wonderful person! A great woman! Who could have done it? Who could have done such a thing?"

Janet's skepticism battled with surprise. When had Carol decided that Mary was so wonderful? Or was it the usual automatic response—a sort of exaggerated *de mortuis nil nisi bonum?*

"You know Dr. Ian Chen, the scientist?"

"Ian? Yes, I know him. What has Ian to do with this?" Suddenly her attention was refocused—all of it on Ian Chen.

"Mrs. Allen was not sympathetic to his work here. She wrote about the harm he was causing."

"Oh no, you don't understand! They were good friends. He encouraged her to write, to raise questions about his work."

A look of disbelief came over the officer's face. "He encouraged her?"

"Yes, yes! You don't understand," she repeated. "In many ways they agreed with each other. They differed only in their ideas about the short-term remedies, not about what had to be done in the long run."

The officer shook his head impatiently. "For us there must be short-term remedies. The time is very bad—and it will get worse."

"Yes, yes." She brushed aside his concern with China's needs. "That may be. That's what Ian . . . Dr. Chen believes. I tell you, they were friends. Good friends. They loved each other."

"Love? They loved each other?"

"Yes, as friends. As old friends. They loved and respected each other."

"And you? What is your relationship to Dr. Chen?"

She stared at him, nonplussed for the moment, wondering how to answer. What *was* her relationship to Ian Chen? But she couldn't think of that now. She closed her eyes and put her head in her hands. "Please. Not now. I can't talk about this anymore. Please leave me alone."

Janet was a little surprised when she saw his lips tighten, as if he was impatient with anyone who delayed the course of his investigation. She remembered how calm he had been when Mrs. Li was murdered. How willing he seemed to be to wait forever until people were moved to speak. Most of the time that seemed to be all he did—wait for something more to happen.

"You'll be able to question her more thoroughly when she's a little calmer," Janet intervened softly. "Why don't you let me take her back to her rooms? You can come there later and talk to her again. You'll probably do much better then."

"Yes, yes," the officer agreed with resignation. "Take her back to her rooms, but tell her not to leave. I will be there shortly, after I have questioned some of the workers here."

Janet put her arm around Carol and walked with her out of the lobby of the hotel and down the steps to the next building. Inside, on the second floor where they had adjacent rooms, the maids were still gossiping excitedly about what had happened. When they saw Janet with Carol they stopped talking and stared silently at them both, watching Janet lead Carol into her suite. She got her to stretch out on the sofa in the sitting room and busied herself making tea with the hot water in the thermos jug on the table in the corner. Somewhere she had read that sugar helped in cases of shock so she added several teaspoons of sugar to the cup from Carol's sugar bowl. She urged her to sit up and drink.

Carol was quiet now, doing everything she was told to do without a murmur of protest. In the aftermath of shock—or perhaps still in it—she seemed to have lost all will of her own, was like a sick child in the hands of a firm adult. What was surprising was that, after such an experience, she still looked so beautiful. Janet, no great beauty to begin with, thought she herself must look a fright.

In a few minutes there was a light knock on the door and Janet opened to one of the maids. "You would like something?" she asked, almost whispering. She tried to peer around Janet to catch a glimpse of Carol lying on the sofa.

"No, thank you. There's nothing. We'll call you if we want something."

"Yes. Call, please," the maid said, not taking her eyes from Carol.

Slowly Janet pushed the door closed, leaving her still standing on the threshold. She was sorry about cutting off her curiosity but she would find out all about it in a very little while—if she hadn't already. The Friendship Hotel hid no secrets from workers or residents. The grapevine here was a marvel unrivaled by modern media of communication.

In a few minutes she opened to a much stronger knock. The officer stood there with a young soldier at his side and a step behind him. "I must ask some questions now," he said to Janet.

"Come in. She may be able to speak to you now. Though what more she can tell you, I can't imagine."

"We will see. She was with Mrs. Allen yesterday." He turned to Carol, who had not moved or opened her eyes.

"There were several of us with Mrs. Allen yesterday," Janet said quickly.

"No," he said. "Miss Walker came to Mrs. Allen's room yester-day afternoon. They were seen—and heard."

Before the dinner? Janet was surprised.

"Miss Walker, at what time did you leave Mrs. Allen's room yesterday?" he asked almost casually, as he looked around for a chair. Seated opposite her, with the soldier behind him, he waited for Carol to respond.

She opened her eyes and struggled to sit up. The stiffness of her jaw tightened her mouth. Her eyelids drooped. In a low voice she answered his question. "We talked until about six o'clock. We were thinking about writing some articles together and I wanted to know everything she knew about the population control pro-gram here in China."

"And you will write about this?"

"I—I don't know. Yes, I think so."

"And about Dr. Chen's work? You will write about that too?"

"Yes, yes, of course. It's all part of the same thing. People have to know everything that's going on so that decisions can be made, not only in China but in other parts of the world."

"You agreed with Mrs. Allen—with what she was trying to do?"

"I . . . I . . . It doesn't matter what I believe!"

"And Dr. Chen? You believe in his work?" he persisted, as if he thought it did matter what she believed.

"Dr. Chen is a sincere scientist who feels his work is important. That's what I want to write about."

"And the Chinese people? You agree with their policies?"

"What has all this to do with Mary's murder? With the horrible . . . horrible . . . ?" Her voice broke.

"We do not know," he said quietly. "But at this time we must question everything. Perhaps in the process some pattern will be-come apparent. What do you say in English? The end of a thread will be revealed and we will follow that thread. A small indication of why someone wanted to kill Mrs. Allen."

Janet grinned to herself at the metaphor. He really was a patient man, so meticulous in his explanations, so gentle. It was no won-

der that suspects spoke to him, hardly realizing what they were
revealing.

Suspects? Was Carol a suspect?

"She must have screamed all the time it was happening," Janet
murmured, almost whispering so that Carol wouldn't hear.

"Perhaps. The deep wounds that finally killed her came later,
after she had been cut repeatedly."

Janet shuddered at the picture of the frantic woman touching
the walls, the bathroom door, grabbing the edge of the bathtub as
she struggled and fought to escape her attacker. The marks of
blood that Carol had described told the story graphically.

"When did it happen? Have you been able to determine the
time?"

He shrugged. "Early this morning, perhaps. After three o'clock.
It is not so certain."

"The front door of the building would have been locked. Who
would have a key besides the worker on duty for the night?"

"The cadre in charge of the hotels. He has a master key that—
he says—is never out of his hands." He smiled a little. "Perhaps
'never' is a little strong. But he does not appear to be one who
leaves the key about carelessly.

"Perhaps Mrs. Allen brought the attacker in with her. Someone
she knew well."

"Her husband, of course," said Janet. "Where is he? Does he
know what's happened?"

"There is no sign of a husband."

Eight

"I GUESS WE ALL ASSUMED, when Ian let them out of the car after the theater, that they both went up together. My God! He'll have to be told." Janet bit her lip; she would *not* jump to the obvious conclusion that Mark had killed his wife and then run.

"The husband applied for a visa a month ago."

Janet felt a spark of admiration for the officer. So calm, so deliberate, almost casual in his inquiries. Yet he had already waded into the morass of bureaucratic red tape and determined that Mary's husband had been issued a visa to come to China. "He arrived yesterday. We all had dinner together last night."

"All?"

"Mary and Mark Allen, Miss Walker, Dr. Chen and I. Why isn't he here? As far as I know, he has no other business in China. Why wouldn't he be here with his wife?"

"He is not registered in the hotel. His record of previous visits reveals that he speaks Chinese as well as his wife did. He could have gone anywhere in Beijing without calling very much attention to himself, since he is able to get about without help."

She heard the note of frustration. Only a short time ago, a Westerner in Beijing would have been spotted very easily. But today the city was host to many foreigners. It would take time to track him down, especially since he had no need to ask for help in getting whatever he needed.

"Mark would never have done anything to Mary!" Janet and

the officer were startled by Carol's vehemence. They had almost forgotten she was there, sitting silent, her head down. "They have . . . had . . . a marvelous marriage. They loved each other dearly." She added the last quietly, as if love required less vehemence, more tenderness.

The officer looked doubtful. "They loved each other dearly? He lives in Tokyo and she spends her time between Beijing and the U.S. and never goes to Tokyo, although both of them are free to travel." It was different for Chinese couples, he implied. They had no choice; being separated was often the only way they could go on working.

"They had an agreement, something they worked out in their lives. It was a very good relationship. They planned that one day they'd live together. But now their work kept them apart and they were satisfied with that."

Apparently Carol hadn't noticed, or chose to ignore, the obvious flaw in that amicable agreement that had been revealed at dinner.

"Is it possible that she brought someone else to her room?" the officer asked. Neither Carol's argument nor her vehemence had convinced him.

"Oh, I don't think . . . Well, it's possible, of course," Janet answered. "But she did seem devoted to her husband and rather straitlaced." She said nothing of her doubts about the marriage. At this point she hardly had enough information to start speculation that might lead the police up a blind alley.

"Straitlaced?"

Janet grinned, considering the source of the old-fashioned idiom that she had never thought about before. "An idiom," she said without explaining. "Puritanical. One who would not bring a lover to her room."

"Not a lover, perhaps. A woman could have killed her."

"So what are we left with? A lover or not a lover, someone she knew or didn't know, someone she brought in with her or who broke in."

"It is not so hopeless as that." He smiled. "We can question the workers to determine when she came in and if she was alone. That should reduce our confusion a little."

Carol began to moan again. "Who could have wanted to do such a thing? Who?"

He answered as if the questions were not just a cry of anguish. "There are many people in China who disagreed with Mrs. Allen's beliefs, who felt she was harming China with what she was writing."

"You think that someone who merely disagreed with her would want to kill her? This seems like such a passionate crime. Could an intellectual disagreement result in so much passion?" Janet mused aloud.

"Who can tell? To someone who believes that his country is in grave danger from a foreigner who hits at the heart of the country's problem . . ."

A foreigner. Of course. The Chinese xenophobia was never far from Chinese passions. How we are never able to forgive our history!

But he was past that thought. "She was considered by many to be a . . . a . . . What is the word? Ah yes, a fanatic. If one believed that a fanatic threatened the stability of the country, if that one who believed was himself a fanatic, he might kill to protect what he cherished."

"Oh, my God!" Carol began to cry again, softly this time, as if she was grieving for a friend. Mary's death was tragedy in itself, but for Carol it might prove disastrous. She would never have the chance to sort out her conflicting loyalties.

"How would someone like that get onto the compound?" Janet asked. No strange Chinese could come through the gates of the Friendship Hotel without being stopped by the soldiers at the gate.

"The people who work here come and go freely."

"You think one of the workers on the compound could have done this?" She was reminded of the tight security in apartment houses at home, where every visitor was stopped and questioned. As if no tenant could ever murder his neighbor or burglarize his neighbor's apartment.

"It is possible. Did we not once agree that anyone, given the circumstances and the conditions that precisely moved him, is capable of murder?"

"There are thousands of people who work here every day. How will you begin to narrow down the numbers?"

"Once before we had such a problem, on an even larger . . . uh . . . compound. Thousands of students and workers, none of whom were ever stopped at the gates. Yet it was only necessary to look at those closest to the victim to discover who had the motive for the killing."

"Yes. The motive. Who would have the motive?" For a moment she forgot the others in the room. A personal motive. One would have to look into her personal life. Her husband . . . "Where can he be?" she wondered aloud.

The phone rang and both women jumped. Carol struggled to get to her feet but Janet said, "Stay put. I'll answer it," and walked across the room to the desk. "Yes?" she said into the phone. "Oh, I imagine it's for you." She held the phone out to the officer. "The man is speaking in Chinese."

He took the phone from her and spoke into it. After a minute or two he said, *"Shi, Shi,"* agreeing, and hung up. "It is the husband," he said. "He has come to his wife at last. We will speak again," he said to Carol.

Janet looked at Carol and then—speculatively—at the officer. Had there been a hint of threat in his voice? Did he have an idea that Carol had murdered Mary? There was nothing definite in his words about when he would be back or what Carol should do in the meantime. Only the calm implication that there might be more she could tell him. He nodded briefly to Janet and left the room.

This officer was, as an individual, very close to the Chinese ideal of what law should be. Although he firmly believed that those found guilty of crimes should be punished, he was not quick to advocate violence as a means either for punishment or for discovering the guilty. Confucius believed in the educability of people, and the Chinese stress on attitude change as a basis for containing deviance is not far from the Confucian idea.

Although the officer used the police and government network to track down pertinent information and uncover certain facts, he was otherwise content to wait out the people related to a crime— wait for them to worry, talk, remember and, finally, betray themselves.

Janet hadn't the patience to be a Confucian. Her first impulse was to follow him so that she could hear what Mary's husband had to say. She was not so cold as to overlook the shock and sorrow Mark would feel when he heard about what had happened to Mary. But somewhere in the back of her mind was the old statistic she had first learned during her work with the Philadelphia police: the odds were largely on the side of someone in the family being the murderer; a wife, murdered, was probably the victim of her husband's rage.

Curiosity or not, she felt obliged to stay a little longer with Carol. It would be a long time before Carol recovered from what she had seen in that hotel room, and right now she needed a friend at her side, whether or not she had murdered Mary herself. The thought came unbidden to Janet's mind. She sounded like a police detective in an archaic mystery story: "At this stage of the game, lady, I suspect everybody."

But what possible reason could Carol have had for killing a woman she hardly knew? One with whom she was contemplating establishing a partnership of sorts? Did the officer have information that she was not aware of? Had he so quickly been able to find a connection between them that might have led to such a dreadful outburst of hate?

Nine

CAROL LAY BACK on the sofa and closed her eyes while Janet sat there, knowing that both of them needed the quiet. Janet wasn't trying to sort things out—not yet. She just let the facts and the ideas come and go in her mind, permitting herself to become familiar with them. When a question arose, she let it circulate among the facts, not trying very hard to answer it. Even for her it was too soon to strain for answers.

Carol's infatuation with Ian Chen had burst upon her, startling her with its white-hot intensity. This beautiful woman—Janet stole a quick glance at her—had gone through the thirty-two years of her life without ever making a serious alliance with a man. Janet had heard this about extremely beautiful women: like very rich men, they often viewed with suspicion bids for their affections. Carol had been absorbed in trying to prove to the world that she was intellectually superior—a superiority that could never be immediately apparent to the people she met. So when a man, introduced to her, tried a tentative overture, she repulsed him, certain that he was attracted to her face, her body. She wanted none of that. Her mind—*that* was attractive. But a mind took time to discover and love. She did not realize that she was too prickly to give a man the necessary time to get to know her.

Ian Chen, beautiful himself, had seemed immediately to appreciate what she had to say. Was interested in her opinions. And his own beauty had broken through the barrier she had kept up for so long. His attention to her fueled a dormant sexual flame. She was very much in love with him. And, at the same time, driven to maintaining her complete independence. Crazy.

Did the police know about Carol and Ian Chen? Did they keep such close tabs on their famous visiting scientist that they knew when he brought a foreign woman to his home?

Had Carol come so late to love that any threat to that love would trigger an abnormal reaction? Had the officer sensed some thread of abnormality in her? He was a very perceptive man, and maybe he had an advantage that she, Janet, didn't have. A person from another culture, perhaps a touch tainted by xenophobia, might be receptive to signs that went right by Janet. They said that anti-Semites had a better average in identifying Jews than unprejudiced people did. Perhaps the same principle was operating here.

Anyhow, Carol was her friend, and Janet knew her own tendency to see her friends as more perfect than they really were.

Mary and her husband probably did have a loving marriage. There had been moments during dinner when they looked at each other very lovingly. Mark had said more than once how happy he was to be back in Beijing. That one outburst of his may have been no more than a momentary irritation that occurred in the best of relationships.

As for the relationship between Mary and Ian, Mary had said, "I love Ian. He's a great man, and a very good man." There was nothing sexual in her admission. Just as Ian himself had said to Carol that he loved Mary as a friend.

Besides, Mary was about her own age, Ian at least twenty years younger. Hah! she laughed at herself. You'd like to think Ian and Mary had something going, wouldn't you? It sort of validated her own claim to youthfulness.

No, Carol had no reason to be jealous of anyone. Ian Chen was obviously in love with her. Surely she was self-confident enough to accept a friendship between her new lover and his old friend without feeling murderous. It was silly even to think that. Unless Carol was a lunatic. Unless her enthusiasm, her brightness and success masked a paranoid killer. Not likely. In real life, paranoia was not so easily masked.

What other reason might the officer have for thinking that Carol was involved in the crime? Well, the murder might have arisen out of altogether professional conflicts—not personal at all. Could Carol have seen Mary as a threat to her lover's work, to his career, and killed for him?

Mary could have been planning systematically to destroy Ian's work. It was all very well to say that Ian saw, in the long run, the need for new solutions to overpopulation. But was it practical for him to accept the risk of losing his funding? Mary was a very popular figure. Maybe she had the power to influence those who supplied Ian's research funds. He had researches going on in the United States as well as in China. Of course the Chinese government paid for most of the work in China—with an assist from the UN—but the American researches were largely funded with American government money. Did she have enough influence to dry up the sources of those grants?

No. Carol wouldn't kill for such a reason. It was more likely that Ian would think of it. Would that model of calm rationality kill if he feared such a possibility?

Ten

WHILE SHE MUSED, she wandered over to the window and watched idly as Mark walked up the path from the gate and was stopped by the soldier at the door of the hotel where his wife had lived. The officer, presumably called from his interrogation of Carol by the guard at the gate so that he could speak to the victim's husband, had been stopped by a maid at the foot of the stairs outside this hotel and stood talking to her.

Janet saw Mark's stance change, and without hearing anything she could see that he was arguing with the soldier, who finally shrugged his shoulders and stood aside to let him into the hotel, following behind.

With a quick glance at Carol, who appeared to have fallen into a doze, Janet ran from the room and down the stairs, yelling to the officer, "We've got to stop him!"

But she got up the outside steps and into the lobby too late. The young soldier had led Mark to the door of Mary's room, opened it and motioned him in. Janet froze at the scream that tore from his throat. She felt her stomach heave and then almost screamed herself at the rush of anger that came over her.

The officer came up behind her and touched her arm tentatively and she turned her fury on him. He stood and listened to her attack, puzzled. "What has happened?"

"You didn't hear him? Your man let him into the room! No preparation! Nothing. Just let him walk in."

He turned on his heel and took the stairs two at a time. Then she heard his icy voice, and the soldier came down, his back ramrod straight, his face red.

Janet went up. Mark was just inside the door of Mary's room, with the officer right behind him. She could see the room from where she stood. She gasped and her knees buckled, and she sagged against the newel post.

For a moment Mark seemed to lose consciousness. The officer caught him around the shoulders and led him out and sat him in a chair in the corridor. After the scream he didn't make another sound. He just sat there as if he had been hypnotized, his eyes wide open, lips slack, no trace of the self-assured man she had met at dinner.

The officer gave an abrupt order to another soldier, who went quickly and came back with a bottle and a glass. The officer tried to drop some of the liquor into Mark's mouth, but it ran over his chin. When Janet put her hand to his face, it felt clammy and she realized he was in profound shock. The officer gave another quick order and the soldier ran to the lobby and the phone. A maid standing there was sent for blankets and Mark was wrapped in them. Then they both stood there looking at him, feeling helpless, not knowing what else to do for the stricken man.

Eventually a doctor came from the clinic on the compound and two soldiers were ordered to lift him and carry him to the clinic, where he was put to bed, still locked in speechlessness.

Any suspicion that anyone might have had that he had killed his wife was at least temporarily suspended. Could a man react so profoundly to anything except an unexpected calamity? If he had been the cause of the blood spattered on the walls and floors, would he have been so shocked by the scene? If he had seen it earlier?

Of course in the heat of passion he could have killed without actually seeing the scene of carnage. It might have been only afterward, when he was faced with it again, that the awfulness of what he had done hit him and sent him catapulting into shock. That was possible for anyone who had killed—anyone, that is, who didn't routinely earn his living by killing.

And who had been closer to Mary than her husband? Who had more opportunity to fall into the million traps of an intimate relationship than a husband? Whose anger was more likely to build and build over years and finally break out in one uncontrollable moment of fury than a husband's?

Preoccupied, Janet wandered out of the building and down the front steps.

"Wang Qu Qing, what are you doing here?"

"I came to see you, Professor."

"I didn't know you were here. How long have you been here?"

"I have come since five minutes."

"Something terrible has happened, Qu Qing. I really can't speak to you right now. I have other things I must do."

"That is fine, Professor. I will go now and come another time."

"I'm sorry, Qu Qing. I hope you don't mind."

"No. It is fine."

"How long did you say you'd been here?"

"I have come now."

Janet watched him as he waved and turned back toward the gate. Had he just come or had he been on the compound since early morning? That would be easy enough to check with the soldiers at the gate. Of course she couldn't do that herself. She would have to suggest to the officer that he do it. But that would mean that she suspected Qu Qing of murdering Mary. She couldn't quite get herself to do that.

Wang Qu Qing was no staunch patriot, but he was committed to the policy of one family, one child. He was also an avid reader of whatever American periodicals he could get his hands on. Had he read Mary's articles? Did he know what she was about? And was he afraid of how she might affect his government's efforts to limit the population?

"China has too many people," he had said to her more than once. She wished the Chinese wouldn't keep saying that. Somehow it seemed to mean that there were too many people living already. Although the authorities might not consciously devalue human life, the belief implicit in the statement could easily encourage official behavior that was contemptuous—or at least careless—of human life. Anyway, was it possible that he could see himself as the savior of the population control program? He probably wanted to follow in Ian's footsteps as desperately as he had once wanted to go to America to study literature. Had he considered Mary Allen a threat to his new idol, and to the important work being done?

She didn't want to believe it. That was the evil spin-off of murder: it made you suspicious of people closest to you, people you cared about. She felt angry with anyone who would murder to solve a human problem. For a fleeting moment she almost believed in capital punishment for the one who had murdered Mary—almost. But that was also a crazy way to solve a human problem.

Eleven

THAT EVENING Janet contemplated a gloomy dinner. The wheels of the Chinese security police ground slowly and invisibly somewhere. Mark remained in the clinic where visitors were turned away with the explanation that he needed time to himself. Carol had also taken to her bed, insisting she wasn't hungry. Janet hadn't seen Dorothy since early afternoon when she had told her about what had happened.

When she walked into the huge dining room, Janet saw the Algerian seated at his usual table at the back. He had known Mary—not only for her writing but personally. What had he said? "I know her well." And she had seen them together. Had he known her well enough to have visited her in her room? He certainly was crazy enough to kill someone and he had been very angry with Mary, seeing her as an analogy for France in Algeria. Just because she had a French mother and was against Chinese policy.

Armand Grisson was almost always alone. After that first time when he had followed her from the counter and sat down with her, she had joined him at breakfast again—just once. Afterward he had acted as if he had never seen her before. Apparently she had not been sympathetic enough with his hatred of black Algerians and of France. Though one didn't have to be crazy to be prejudiced against black people, his kind of prejudice *was* craziness. To give up a country that one obviously loved rather than work cooperatively with another racial group was the kind of psychosis that was getting less and less sympathy in the world.

She brought her plate over to his table. "Do you mind if I join you?" she asked.

"No, no. Not at all," he said cordially, as if he hadn't been snubbing her for weeks.

"I . . . er . . . noticed you on your motorcycle," she said tentatively, hoping she would strike, if not a happy note, at least a neutral one.

"Ah, yes. You like my motorcycle? It is wonderful to ride her. I can go everywhere!"

"Um . . . er . . . yes. I'm sure you can."

"Perhaps one day I will take you to ride," he offered.

She suppressed a shudder. The thought of riding on that thing made her teeth ache. "That would be nice." She smiled weakly, praying he wouldn't suggest a ride in the very near future. "Er . . . You knew Mary Allen, didn't you?" she said quietly, hoping she would not provoke an explosion.

But apparently he was not feeling explosive at the moment. The motorcycle was making him too happy. "Yes, I knew her. When I first came here we spoke French together. She spoke very well. She told me about Beijing."

"You were friends?"

For the first time she saw what resembled a smile on his face. It was not a pleasant smile. It had something mean in it. "She thought she could use me for her own purposes. She wanted advance copies of news that would appear in the *China Daily*—advance copies of government announcements. But who knows who was being used, eh?"

Such advance information would have enabled her to publish her own counterarguments and, perhaps, take the steam out of the official statements when they finally appeared in print.

"You gave her what she wanted?"

He had that smile again. "She thought I did so—for a time. Then she realized that I was not a fool. But by then we were very close and it was too late."

Janet had already seen evidence of Mary's way of using people to make her own life comfortable, to achieve her own goals. She had done it with charm, in getting Ian to be her trusting friend; with aggressive pressure, in convincing Carol to work with her. Now Armand was implying that she had used sex to get him to help her learn in advance what the Chinese government was planning.

Janet's look showed her perplexity. "Too late?"

"I had evidence of her betrayal and I told her to leave China."

"*You* told her to leave?"

"She would have to leave or I would inform the authorities."

"When was she planning to leave China?"

"Soon, soon. She would have been gone soon. She knew there was no other way."

"She refused to leave, didn't she? You couldn't convince her."

"It doesn't matter now." He gritted his teeth, slammed his spoon down on the table and almost ran from the dining room.

Janet blew a soundless whistle. She'd hate to have him *really* angry at her.

She was delighted to see Dorothy come in with John. They joined her at the table.

"We knew you'd be in," Dorothy greeted her. "We were going to wait dinner for you."

"Oh, thanks. I'm so glad to see you."

"Are you all right?"

"Sure. As all right as anyone could be. It's hard to believe we all had dinner together only yesterday evening."

"I looked in on Carol. She's in bad shape."

"Yes. Walking in on that . . . that . . . It was terrible for her."

"And for Mary Allen's husband. How is he feeling?"

"He's in the hospital. I haven't seen him."

"Poor man."

They were quiet for a while, depressed by it all.

"I wonder if you've ever met him, John. He works in Tokyo too."

"Tokyo's a big city, love."

"Oh, I'm sure foreigners who speak the same language all tend to meet sooner or later."

"It's not like Beijing. There are many more foreigners in Tokyo. And people all dress in Western clothes. Foreigners don't stick out so."

"His name is Mark Allen. He . . ."

"The banker?" he said. "Oh yes. I know him."

"You do? He's Mary Allen's husband. You know, the woman who writes all those things about China's population control." And then she added, "The woman who was murdered."

"Wife? He's got a wife?"

"Yes, what of it? You say that as if wives were rare in your part of the world."

He grinned and chucked her under the chin. "Not in *my* part of the world. But I thought they were in Allen's part of the world."

"What do you mean?" Janet asked. But she thought she already knew the answer. There had been something in Mark's manner toward Ian that had caught Janet's attention. Some special eagerness when Ian talked to him; the way his body leaned ever so slightly toward the scientist, as if drawn by an irresistible attraction.

John's answer was no surprise. "He's homosexual." He shrugged. "He's well known in Tokyo—or at least his dinners are. Only men invited. Terrific food."

"You've been?" Dorothy seemed ready to tease him but his matter-of-factness took the steam out of her impulse.

"Yes. I was curious. And I'd heard the food was great. No lie."

"I wonder if his wife knew," Dorothy said.

"Well, at dinner last night there was an undercurrent of animosity between them."

How could Mary not have known—every time her husband looked at Ian? What *was* that marriage all about? If Mary really was not as ingenuous as she appeared at first, if she made a career out of using people for her own purposes, maybe this kind of marriage suited her. To have the convenience of a husband, with all the surface respectability this afforded, especially in China, and at the same time to be free to travel about and make her various types of contacts. In this marriage, there might have been a question of who was using whom.

"Was she involved with Ian Chen at all?" Dorothy asked.

Janet shrugged. "She made a point of denying it. At the time I believed her. But now I have my doubts. She begins to emerge as a rather self-centered person, demanding whatever she needed without caring who got hurt.

"At first I thought she had worked hard to build a good relationship with Ian because she liked him as a friend even though she disagreed with his philosophy. But now I'm less inclined to accept that picture."

"You think she was writing purposely to hurt him?"

"No-o-o. Not really. I think she believed what she wrote. But it would be more consistent with what I'm finding out about her to believe she really didn't give a damn what happened to Ian or his work because of the kind of publicity she gave them. She expected him to go on being her friend no matter what she did— because *she* wanted it. Maybe she wanted more—I don't know. Maybe once they *were* more to each other."

"What effect do you think she had on him?"

Janet shook her head. "He's a pretty strong person—knows who he is and just what he's about. I imagine no one could manipulate him—make him do something he didn't want to do."

She looked up to see Carol walk briskly into the dining room. She had brushed her hair and put on lipstick and looked as if nothing serious had happened recently.

"Carol," Dorothy began. But she was interrupted.

"It's a beautiful evening, isn't it?" Carol asked brightly. "I thought I'd get out now and enjoy the evening and then stay up at night to work on my articles. I don't feel a bit sleepy."

"You look great," Dorothy told her. She didn't mention that not half an hour earlier Carol had looked ready for a hospital bed.

Janet just eyed her speculatively. There was something manic in the exaggerated brightness, in the quick, birdlike movements of her head and hands as she spoke. She hoped Carol wasn't heading for a monumental crash.

They were all startled by the sudden appearance again of Armand Grisson. He sat himself at their table and motioned peremptorily to the waitress to take his order, as if he hadn't just eaten. Maybe, Janet thought, he had left before he'd finished his dinner.

"Hi," Janet said uncomfortably.

He nodded to her and to Dorothy, who looked at him with a half smile. He ignored Carol. And he spoke to John. "You are here to work in China?"

John eyed him impassively without answering. When the silence began to bother her, Janet introduced the two men. "Mr. Brigham is just visiting," she explained.

"Good. China has sufficient of foreigners," the Algerian announced.

"Why are *you* here?" John asked him.

"I help China. I do not want to change her."

"Very commendable."

The sarcasm was lost on Grisson. "The American writer has been murdered. The Chinese are able to protect themselves from those who would betray their country."

"You think a Chinese murdered her?" Janet asked.

"Who else could come and go in the hotel without being noticed?" he asked rhetorically, and attacked the food the waitress brought.

There was silence for a while as they ate. Then Janet said slowly, "Two things bother me about it. One, why did no one respond to the screaming? It must have been heard—and by more than one person. The other is, how did the murderer get away without calling attention to his bloodstained clothes?"

"Maybe his room is right nearby—in the same corridor as Mary's room," John suggested.

Dorothy shook her head. "That doesn't seem likely. There are only tourists on that floor. As a matter of fact, except for us, there are only tourists in the whole building." She dismissed the idea that an unknown tourist could have committed the murder.

Janet agreed. "It's pretty farfetched to think that someone traveling through China suddenly found a motive to kill her."

"Unless it was just a random killing—a lunatic."

"That's always possible, I suppose. But the odds are all against it. A stranger might go berserk in a public place and hit out blindly at everyone in the vicinity. But to be admitted to some-one's room, kill that person, and then leave, covering his tracks—that's too unlikely a combination of insanity and rationality to be a random killing. Though the murderer may be insane, it's an insanity triggered by the relationship with the victim. There must be a motive that can be understood—even if it isn't condoned."

"You speak as if you have an idea who it could be."

"No, not really," she said thoughtfully. And then, as if she spoke without volition, the words coming out of her automati-cally—the way words sometimes come from the pen of a writer, "The clothing. The blood and the clothing."

"What do you mean?" Dorothy asked.

Janet shook herself as if coming out of a trance. "Damned if I know," she said. "I'll have to give it some thought."

"There is nothing to think about," Grisson announced between mouthfuls.

"You believe you know how she was killed?" she asked him.

"Yes." Then, curiously, "She was a woman who saw only her own needs, only what she wanted for herself. Even I was fooled."

"She fooled you? How?"

"It does not matter now. She has been stopped."

What a world of brutality in that short sentence! Janet's appe-tite was gone. She thought it useless to respond.

But Carol wouldn't let it go by. "You're crazy! She never did a thing to you! You're making it all up."

Before he could answer, Janet averted a fight by picking up on what Carol had said earlier. "You're planning to go ahead with the articles?"

"Yes, of course. Why not? You didn't think I agreed to do them just because Mary wanted me to, did you? I *do* have a mind of my own, you know."

"I never doubted that," Janet answered dryly.

"You're going to write about the work your Ian Chen is doing? Won't he mind your raising questions?" Dorothy asked.

"Why should he? He didn't mind when Mary did it. Anyhow, whether he minds or not, I have no intention of changing my plans."

As if she had never had any doubts. As if the idea had been hers all along.

Grisson had finished eating and departed as abruptly as he had come.

"I wonder what she did to him," Dorothy mused.

"He's mentioned before that he knew her. Something about her mother being French."

"Do you think they were lovers? With her husband what he is . . . ?"

Janet shrugged.

"Maybe he did it." John grinned. "He's crazy enough."

"I don't think so," Janet said. "He'd have been spotted going into the hotel. He has an apartment on the other side of the compound. And even if he had a good reason for entering the hotel—to visit a tourist or something—the workers would have seen him."

Carol had been sitting there listening. Her face had gradually become very flushed and her breathing labored. "What are you all saying about Mary?" she almost hissed. "What are you implying? She was a wonderful person. Everyone loved her. She was honest and she had integrity. And I'm going to tell the world what she believed—what that editor of hers never let her say." Her breathing was quick and shallow and her eyes sparkled. She looked ready for battle.

"Well," Janet said, "maybe Ian is the one man who can live with having the woman he loves seen by the public as his adversary. If any man can do it, he can." It was meant to soothe Carol, but it didn't work.

"He'll just have to," she said. "I make my own decisions. Just as Mary did."

Maybe shock tactics would bring her down from her unnatural high. "What's between you and Ian goes far beyond a loving friendship that can survive the batterings of opposing points of view. He and Mary didn't have a bed as part of the field of battle."

Carol gasped. For a second she seemed about to deny hotly that what went on in that bed had any bearing on her work. Finally she said stiffly, "In bed or out, Ian must accept me as an independent person, as someone who has a mind of her own. If he can't take me as I am, he will just have to walk away."

"Where is the gorgeous Dr. Chen? You should meet him, John. He's so-o-o handsome!"

"Are you trying to destroy my self-confidence?" The way he asked that, flatly, with no emotion, demonstrated how little bothered he was by Dorothy's exaggerated admiration for another man. It broke the tension at the table and made the three women laugh.

"I tried to get him at the lab before I came in," Carol said, "but the one man still working there didn't speak English. And he's not at home." A worried frown appeared on her face. "I can't imagine why he didn't call me. He must have heard about what happened."

"The police may be talking to him. He's the only one who can tell them about Mary. Her husband can't talk yet."

"You don't think they suspect *Ian* of . . . ?"

"No, of course not," Janet reassured her. But she wasn't all that sure herself. Ian Chen was a complex man. His approach to problems required some analysis before she could understand him. The security officer would recognize this and take his time in questioning the scientist.

"I'm sure you're right. He's quite capable of handling the police."

"*Handling* the police?" Janet asked. "Why would that be necessary? He has nothing to hide." Her statement ended on a slightly questioning note.

"I know he hasn't!" Carol's emphasis sounded perilously close to hysteria. "Mary was important to him; he'd never h-hurt her." Then, switching focus abruptly, "He knows I'm perfectly fine. He'll call when he can."

There it was again—the unnatural drive to be seen as independent, totally in control, needing no one's comfort or support. Janet thought that if *her* lover had not rushed to reach her after so devastating an experience she would have been furious. So, she thought, would most people.

Twelve

"HE IS LEAVING the country."

Janet goggled at the officer. "You're letting him leave? Just like that?"

"Pardon?"

"Er . . . uh . . . nothing." She recovered her cool and attempted a reasoning disappointment at not being able to see Ian. "I was just curious to know what his reaction is to his friend's death. I understand he hasn't been to visit Mark Allen in the hospital."

"He was at home all last night when Mrs. Allen was murdered, he says. Do you have cause to suspect he may not be telling the truth?"

"No, no. Certainly not. I—it's just that . . . Mark Allen is also his friend. I can't help wondering why he avoids seeing him— even if it's only to express his sympathies."

The officer nodded. "Perhaps he suspects his friend—or is certain that he is the one."

Janet just looked at him. That was exactly what she was thinking. Was Ian avoiding Mark because he hated the idea of looking at the face of the man who had murdered Mary?

"Why is Dr. Chen leaving?" she asked.

"There is a crisis in one of his studies at home. He goes to help those who work in the laboratory in San Francisco. He will return shortly."

She smiled. "In America he would not have been permitted to leave until the investigation was over."

"Dr. Chen is a great man," he said. He barely restrained a smile. Just as he had once reminded her that good people lie, they were both also aware that great people kill. "He will return to China," he said confidently. "Even if he should want to do so, a man of his stature would find no place in the world to hide himself."

She thought of the murderers with "stature" who had found refuge in countries that could profit from their special skills, that were happy to overlook their crimes. But she said nothing.

"Have you learned anything more about the people involved with Mrs. Allen?"

Though he raised his eyebrows at the bluntness of the question, he also smiled fondly at the outspoken American. "I am afraid," he said, "that you are probably in a better position to find things out. You speak regularly with the people here; they are not so candid with the police as they are with other foreigners."

"Oh, have you already concluded that the murderer is a foreigner?"

"No. But perhaps someone here knows something that he is reluctant to talk about. He might more readily tell you about it."

She felt guilty, as if he was reminding her that she herself might not always be completely candid with the police. At the moment she thought that Mark's homosexuality—or maybe bisexuality—was irrelevant. There was no point in mentioning it to the law officer of a culture where it might even be punishable by death. How quickly the Chinese had changed their attitude on this, she thought. As late as the beginning of the twentieth century both homosexuality and bisexuality had been widely accepted. Now China was far behind even the United States on that one.

"Do you know the Algerian?" she asked abruptly.

"The one with the motorcycle?"

"He makes himself noticed, doesn't he?" Anyone who bought such an odd machine in Beijing would be known to the police. He probably had had to move through a sea of red tape before he could buy it and get a license to use it. Even before he could find someone who had one to sell.

"What has he to do with the murder?"

"Well, he knew Mary Allen. He certainly resented her."

"We have no knowledge of this." He said it almost triumphantly, as if his impulse to collaborate with Janet was now justified. "What was his relation to her?"

"It's not very clear to me. He thought she was an enemy of China. Somehow he saw her opposition to China's population control policies as similar to what happened in his own country. The French government decided that the Moslem Algerians had a right to control the government of Algeria. He feels his country was betrayed by outsiders—just as China was being betrayed by an outsider."

"You think he would kill for this?"

She shrugged. "I think there's more to it than that. His behavior suggests a personal involvement with Mary. Do you know anything of his movements during the night of the murder?"

"We had no reason to ask about them. But we will now."

She felt a small pleasure at the thought. Anyone who disturbed the peace of the world the way he did deserved to have his own peace disturbed.

"He bothers me. He seems to have shifted his animosity from Mary to Carol. He's not a very stable character."

"Miss Walker? Why is he angry with her?"

"Oh, of course, you wouldn't know. She's planning to write about Dr. Chen's work. She's rather a well-known writer in the United States."

"Did she agree with Mrs. Allen? Will she write the same things?"

"Frankly, I'm not sure. She herself doesn't seem to be very clear about what approach she will take. But she certainly made it clear that she admired Mrs. Allen and respected the work she did."

"Does the Algerian know this?"

"Yes. He was at dinner with us when we talked about it." Now that she had said it so baldly, a frisson of fear ran up her spine. She was not at all happy about that man.

They strolled companionably toward the building where Mary had had her room. They had not walked like this for three years, and it came to them again how much pleasure they took in each other's company.

"So," he said. "You have returned to China. Have you decided to make your home here?" The twinkle in his eyes betrayed him. He was teasing her.

"I certainly felt that I was coming home. It was so good to see old friends. It's too bad that we must meet again over murder."

"Yes. We have so few murders in Beijing, yet you seem to . . . uh . . . turn up each time."

"Well, at least this time there's no question of my being a suspect. That was not a comfortable situation to be in." That gets me the prize for understatement, she thought.

She saw Carol some distance away and nodded goodbye to the officer. As she came closer, she saw that Carol was involved in an intense conversation with someone. She appeared about to disintegrate again. She held a sheet of paper in her hand and it fluttered with the trembling of her body like a thing alive. The person was Pan Lin, one of Ian Chen's lab technicians. Janet recognized him as the young man who had smilingly hovered at Ian's elbow while he showed them around the installation. Now he wasn't smiling. He looked worried.

"What's wrong?" Janet asked.

Carol looked at her blankly and ran up the steps and into the hotel. Pan Lin and Janet looked after her in consternation.

"She is very unhappy," he announced at last.

"I can see that," she answered dryly. "Did you bring a note from Dr. Chen?"

"Yes. He returns to his home for a short time. Perhaps his workers have made a . . . er . . . breakthrough."

"That would be exciting—if all the work you're doing is finally successful."

"Yes. Very good for China. Dr. Chen is a great scientist. His own people know this too."

Her mind mostly on Carol, she asked absently, "Would you like to visit the United States sometime? Perhaps work there with Dr. Chen?"

"I have been to U.S. with Dr. Chen. I have seen many labs. Also

I have met his friends and his family." His face beamed. He had already forgotten Carol's agitation.

"How nice." She had to get to Carol and try to help her.

"We were to San Francisco. The streets made us feel as in a boat when we were in the car. Dr. Chen told me a Chinese poet in America wrote about this."

"Chiang Yee," Janet murmured.

"Dr. Chen has many children in San Francisco."

That focused her attention firmly on Pan Lin. "Many children? I didn't know Dr. Chen was married."

"Not married, but many children. From all countries."

She listened to his description of a visit he had made with his mentor:

They drove for about half an hour until they came to a quiet street on a hill. Ian pulled up in front of a row of bayed houses so characteristic of San Francisco architecture. A small child opened when he knocked and grinned at Ian before he began to yell for Anna. "It's Ian! It's Ian! He's coming on the picnic! Anna, it's Ian!" Then he ran into the recesses of the house, leaving the door open.

Ian urged Pan Lin inside and shut the door behind them. The young man wondered who this family was and how the five-year-old had gotten to know the great Dr. Chen so well that he called him by his first name and was apparently beside himself with excitement and joy at the visit. Ian himself was laughing with what appeared to be joy as great as the child's.

Suddenly, in the small entrance foyer, there were children everywhere—some with jet-black hair and oriental features who might have been fathered by Ian, others blond and blue-eyed, and at least two black children. They all laughed and talked at once as they converged on the visitors, grabbing at Ian at whatever level they stood until they threatened to knock him over with their enthusiasm.

Pan Lin felt uncomfortable, the way one does upon coming into the home of strangers, uncertain of welcome, diffident because he was not a part of this family and Dr. Chen was. Understanding the language but not the relationships.

But it wasn't for very long. Ian drew him into the laughing, shouting circle. Somehow they all moved out of the foyer into a large living room. He managed to look around him, taking in the warmth and homeyness of the flowered upholstery, the softness of plants everywhere, the smiles on the faces of these healthy, happy children. One child, no more than three, ran to Ian and clasped his legs. Ian bent and swung him into the air, laughing with him. Throughout the visit he held the little boy in his arms.

"Ian, how good to see you! I thought you were still in China!" The woman who came into the room greeted him with a hug. She was small, dressed in jeans and a T-shirt. Her blond hair was cut short. She looked both comfortable and competent, not at all put out by the noisiness of the children or the unexpected arrival of guests.

"This is Pan Lin," Ian introduced him. "And this is Anna Singman."

"We miss Ian when he's away. The kids keep asking when he's coming back."

Pan Lin cast a sidelong glance at him. A surprising side of the scientist. What was he here? Uncle? Father?

But no, here came the father. Paul Singman was just as pleased to see him. They shook hands like good friends, grinning at each other wordlessly.

Two more children came down the stairs; he could hear the clumps of their feet before they appeared. One was about six, one seven. Surely Anna Singman had not given birth to all of them! A teenager came in from outside and tossed a load of books on the table. He also shook hands with Ian, fighting the need to be cool with the impulse to hug the visitor. They ended up holding each other's right hands and half hugging, half slapping each other on the back.

"We weren't expecting you!" the boy said several times, as if this visit was a hoped-for gift.

Finally they were all sitting—the children on the floor and chair arms. There seemed to be dozens, most of them between the ages of three and ten or eleven. But when the noise and movement settled down somewhat Pan Lin thought there were only eight or nine. What was this?

Still bewildered by the laughing and talking in a language not his own and by the diversity of races, at one point he said in an aside to Anna, "All these children . . ." His voice petered out.

"Oh," Anna gestured airily, "most of them are Ian's doing."

Pan Lin's eyes widened. He knew Ian was a genius but he doubted that was enough to explain all of them. "He could not . . ."

Anna threw her head back and laughed. "He could if he wanted to!" she was eventually able to say. Then she sobered. "You don't know about Ian?" she asked. "All this is provided by him. These were unwanted children. Would you believe it? Unwanted! He bought this home, gave us a chance to care for them. He's a re-markable man."

"Yes," Pan Lin agreed. "A remarkable man."

"Two of them are our own. Paul and I haven't been entirely idle," she added mischievously. "The rest have been brought here by parents and grandparents who . . . who . . ." She was at a loss for words, the idea too gross, too unbelievable for her to express.

"You have adopted them?"

"Oh no. They still belong to their parents, who will one day realize what they've missed. We just care for them, bring them up to know that they matter, that they're important. One day they may meet their parents and it will be as equals, people who are confident of their own worth, with no bitterness and with the ability to love. No one will ever again be able to say about them that they were expendable."

As she listened Janet began to understand a little more about Ian Chen, about the meaning of his life. He was committed, not to the idea that there were too many people in the world, but to the belief that ways must be found to make all people comfortable in this finite world. That was why he was able to encourage a Mary Allen even while he worked to discover better ways of limiting populations.

Such a man could never kill anyone, could he?

"Thanks for telling me about Dr. Chen, Pan Lin."

He nodded. "I will go now." He bowed and turned to walk down the path toward the gate, and she hurried into the hotel to see if Carol was all right.

Thirteen

CAROL HAD RECOVERED by the time Janet got her to open her
door. She said she would have an early night and Janet left her,
but not without misgivings. The rapid mood switches were disturbing to the older woman. She got the feeling that Carol was out
of control, that the periods of apparent calm were achieved by
enormous effort of will and could not be maintained for very long.
And she felt powerless to do much that was helpful, except continue to express her willingness to listen if Carol wanted to talk.

She extracted a promise that Carol would join her the next day
for a quiet afternoon in Bei Hai Park. Sunday was everyone's time
for parks and picnics. Perhaps the peaceful setting and the atmo-
sphere of relaxation would encourage her to express whatever was
upsetting her, and so relieve some of the pressure she was under.

But right now Janet wanted to think, and she did that best
while walking. She preferred walking in city streets, where people
and shopwindows and such minor distractions as getting across a
road without being run down afforded a counterpoint to her
thoughts and served to make them more acute. But she would
have to make do with the paths of the compound, almost deserted
now in the quiet night. To walk outside the gate, where there were
no sidewalks and no streetlights, was not at all an attractive prospect.

As she walked she was occasionally aware of the echoing sound
of her heels on the pavement. She passed the tourist hotel and

looked up at it. How had the murderer got out in his blood-spattered clothing? Just walked out? If it was three in the morning, he might have risked not meeting anyone. But if it was four or five, he would surely have been seen. Everyone in China went fast asleep by ten o'clock. The place was deserted then. Even the person assigned to the lobby desk disappeared into a small room behind the desk. The hotel door was locked, and it took considerable effort to get it opened if one happened to return home after ten o'clock. The desk person slept soundly.

When, exactly, had the murder occurred? The staff was usually up and stirring about by five-thirty in the morning. Would there be an autopsy and efforts made to determine the exact time of death? Such determinations, she knew, were far from exact even in ideal scientific circumstances. Facilities available to the Chinese police for dealing with dead bodies were far from ideal. They used the hospitals for whatever tests they needed and, understandably, doctors who were always in short supply were more concerned with the living who crowded in for treatment.

Maybe whoever had done it did, after all, live in the hotel and was able to duck into his own room and change immediately. Would it be worthwhile to search every room for traces of blood? For bloody clothes?

Perhaps one of the tourists *did* know Mary. Someone from the United States who knew about her work and wanted to stop her. Long-distance travel, with its increase of frustration and lowering of controls, might have pushed a traveler off the rails. Would it be necessary to interrogate everyone in the hotel before eliminating all the tourists as suspects?

Walking back toward her own building in the dark, she was unexpectedly afraid. She'd never before been afraid to walk on the paths of the compound after dark, but now all kinds of things around seemed menacing. She suddenly was aware that there were no streetlights. Generally the paths were lighted by the windows and lobbies of the surrounding buildings, but it was late and most of the lights had been put out and the residents gone to bed. She looked up and saw a figure outlined against the dimness from the few lights still on. An arm was upraised, ready to strike. She was paralyzed with fear, unable to move.

The figure was in the bicycle shed, a gimcrack structure of a roof on thin posts, without walls. It rose out of the mass of bicycles propped against wooden rails, looming toward her. She could see the knife in its hand as it came down in a stabbing motion. The same knife that had killed Mary?

Abruptly she found her feet, if not her voice, and began to run frantically. She heard running behind her and forced herself to run faster, even though she was already gasping for breath. Up the steps of the hotel, she slammed through the door and banged it shut behind her, in the face of someone who was right on her heels. She almost fell over to the desk behind which stood the clerk staring at her in surprise, shocked at her gasps and dishevelment. This kind of behavior from the foreign professor!

The door she had slammed shut opened and Armand Grisson came in. "You run from me, eh? Why do you run from me? I am not to be spoken to? There is something not right about speaking to me? You wish to look down on me because I am Algerian?"

She gaped at him, unable to reconcile his indignant scolding with what she had imagined was coming after her. Finally he stopped for breath.

"Oh, for goodness' sake, Armand. I didn't know it was you. Why didn't you say something?"

She didn't believe he had just waved to her. She didn't believe he just wanted her to speak to him. There was something menacing about the man—something crazy menacing. She didn't trust him. He *could* have killed Mary. He could kill anybody. She pushed from her mind for the moment the admission that chagrin at her own precipitous panic was partly the reason for her anger and was making her fasten on reasons that would make her less ashamed of herself for running.

"You must not reveal who murdered that woman," Armand commanded. "If you have information, do not give it to the police. It is better that she is silenced and China will have peace."

Such egocentric arrogance was the absolute limit! First he had tried to pressure Mary into leaving China, and now this. Would

Carol be next, since he knew she was going to take up the writing where Mary had stopped? Her anger boiled over. "Don't tell me what I should do or should not do! I'll do as I damn well please!" she yelled at him.

He took a step back in surprise. Those who were accustomed to riding roughshod over people's feelings, who were routinely rude and made outrageous demands on virtual strangers, were often taken aback at rudeness—or even explicit candor—in others. He turned away and disappeared as abruptly as he usually did.

The maids were surprised when she asked them for several of their homemade mouse-catchers, but she didn't bother to explain. She hoped they would assume that she had seen a lot of mice and had changed her mind about being too disgusted to live with those devices under her furniture. When they brought two of the large slabs of cardboard smeared with sticky stuff and dotted with bits of food, she felt sick to her stomach. And she asked for three more. They stared at her. Where was she going to put them all? There was just the single bed, the desk, the sofa and two easy chairs. Was she going to leave them out where everyone could see them? Fortunately they asked their questions in Chinese and she was able to shrug and imply that she didn't understand what they were saying. She literally didn't understand, but the puzzled expressions on their faces were clear; she would have asked the same questions of anyone who had asked her for those things.

Later, when she was sure everyone was asleep and the floor maids had left their seats in the corridor, she carefully placed four of the cardboards in a row outside her door, so that anyone coming up to the door in the dim night light would surely step into them. She put one more just inside the door, hoping she wouldn't get up in the morning with a catch of mice helplessly stuck and struggling to free themselves. She didn't think she could stand that.

She got into bed, feeling a little safer in her room with a murderer loose. Perhaps a murderer who believed she had information that could lead to his apprehension.

Fourteen

IT WAS A PERFECT DAY. Not even a mouse had lost his freedom or his life, and Janet's fears of the night before felt foolish, unfounded. Bei Hai Park was crowded as usual with Chinese from Beijing and the countryside. Here and there one could easily identify the foreign tourists—Japanese men in black pants and white open-necked shirts busy with their cameras; Westerners, probably Europeans, the women in flowered print dresses. But mostly there were Chinese, strolling, sitting on the edges of the lake peeling apples, running after small children. It was noisy but peaceful. No one had a destination to reach, an itinerary to cover. Dorothy had come along, leaving her guest to recover from delayed jet lag.

The sound of the argument rose above the din of cheerful noise. Two men had stopped on the path, squared off and were shouting at each other. The people around them also stopped and stood watching calmly, commenting smilingly to their companions.

The two men were young, unremarkable in appearance. Except that one held what looked like a heavy bat—a length of solid dark wood that he was using to lean on. He raised it above his head, and suddenly it was a threatening weapon. The other man put up his hands—half fearful, half ready to fight. The crowd closed in, but it was not clear why. Were they interested in getting a better view of the fight? Were they trying to summon up group courage to intervene before one of the men was badly hurt? Or was it some kind of mindless, instinctive drawing together to close out the world and let the drama unfold without interference?

Janet, Carol and Dorothy were trapped in the crush behind them, unable to get away, too close to the impending violence for safety. They huddled together, appalled at what was happening, feeling themselves pushed nearer to the two men.

The stick came down, but the other's upraised hands stopped it before it reached his head, and they struggled, silently now, for possession. Janet could hear their gasping breath, see the sweat on their flushed faces, feel the fascination even while she was frightened and repelled. Carol, too, seemed drawn to the silently struggling men, because she moved precipitously toward them just as the heavy stick came down on her head.

The scream from many throats jerked her back just in time.

Silently the two men melted into the crowd, the wooden weapon abandoned in the circle. Everyone began to talk at once.

"What's the matter with you?" Janet yelled. "Are you trying to get yourself killed?" She could feel the sweat on her back under her dress and her knees were weak.

"I don't know." Carol tried to catch her breath. "I don't know what's the matter with me."

"That wasn't your fault," Dorothy protested. "Someone must have pushed you."

"He just missed me. I could feel it brush my hair."

"My God! If that plank had hit you it would have taken the top of your head off."

"Please," Janet implored. "Not so graphic."

"He looked as if he wanted to hit you."

"What? Don't be silly. Why would he want to do a thing like that?"

"Oh no. I didn't mean that. I'm sure it was just an accident."

Janet said nothing, picturing again the way the man had half turned from his opponent as the stick descended toward Carol's head. What had she yelled: "Are you trying to get yourself killed?"

"It all happened so fast." Carol was still breathless. "I thought . . . I thought . . ."

"Come along, let's get out of here." Janet herded them both through the press of people around them. They walked quickly to the open square near the entrance to the park, where vendors sold ice cream and sodas. There was an empty bench and Dorothy and Carol sat while Janet brought them orange drinks. They grimaced as they drank the sickly sweet stuff.

They sat for a while saying nothing, only making faces with each sip, until Janet began to giggle, partly with reaction to the threat of violence and partly at the picture they made—a sort of variation on the no-evil monkeys. Carol caught it too. Dorothy looked at them both for a moment with a show of disdainful indignation, resisting a loss of dignity. Then she whooped and laughed louder than the others.

At a respectful distance from these nutty foreigners a crowd of Chinese people gathered in puzzled watchfulness. Some of them began to smile. Most of the children laughed too. Finally the three women dried their eyes.

"Let's have some lunch. John's jet lag will keep him sleeping all afternoon."

"Good idea. Where?"

"We passed a restaurant on the way in," Dorothy remembered. "Let's try it."

They smiled to the crowd and walked out of the park. The brightness of the day and the amiability of all the people enjoying their holiday kept memory of the incident at bay—at least for the moment.

They settled down in the restaurant, which apparently catered to a Chinese clientele. It was late for lunch. Most of the patrons had already gone, leaving the tables strewn with fish bones and empty rice bowls. Nobody hurried to clean their table, so they found a damp cloth on a ledge that held chopsticks and spoons and cleared the table themselves, brushing the debris to the floor and stacking the bowls at the far end of the table. A waitress sauntered over, took their order and accepted payment, and strolled away in the general direction of the kitchen. In casual contact, strangers were charming and helpful to foreigners, but both the Chinese and foreigners were treated equally by clerks and waiters—equally badly. It was difficult to determine if the attitude indicated complacency because people rarely were fired, or if it was resentment at the need to do work that was considered menial. Or maybe it was the same supercilious arrogance displayed by civil service workers around the world—in a place where almost everyone was employed by the government.

At any rate, when the food was finally brought, it was delicious. They ate quickly, as if the experience had speeded up all movement, all functions. Or as if gorging themselves would tamp down the fear that threatened to overwhelm.

From the length of the restaurant away, a young woman left several companions at her table and came purposefully to stand facing Carol. She began to speak in rapid Chinese, in a low voice. Gradually, as she went on and on, her voice rose until it became clear—even though the three women could understand nothing of what she was saying—that she was furious with Carol.

They looked at each other, mystified, and then at the other people, hoping to see someone who could tell them what this was all about. But the waitresses clustered against a wall and the few patrons in the room just listened intently. No one responded to their questioning looks.

The woman continued to shout until she ran out of breath—or words. She stopped, took a deep shuddering sigh and stalked out of the restaurant. They stared silently after her.

"What the hell . . . ?" Carol spluttered.

Dorothy pursed her lips and whistled silently. "It's our day for Down With Foreigners, isn't it?"

"No," said Janet thoughtfully. "This is not the way xenophobia works in China. Carol, did she look familiar to you?"

"I don't think so. Have you seen her before?"

Janet frowned, trying to recall. A picture of Ian Chen in a white coat came to her. And the laboratory with busy researchers bent over their tables. Except one. One who stared at Ian's back while he talked to the visitors; one whose eyes followed him as he moved about the room. "I think she's one of Ian Chen's researchers. I'm pretty sure I saw her in his lab."

"What's she got against you?" Dorothy asked.

Carol shrugged. "I don't know."

"She looked furious about *something*. Maybe you cut her out with the eminent Dr. Chen."

"You think she and Ian . . . ?"

"It's possible. If you've had no contact with her, he's the only connection between the two of you."

"Not exactly," Janet said. "There's the work they're doing. Maybe she thinks Carol will interfere with it."

"Why, that's ridiculous. I would never stand in the way of Ian's work."

Janet's eyebrows rose at the vehemence of the denial. It was too much protest; the doubt about what she was planning to do must be bothering her. "Maybe she's afraid that raising questions about the program will weaken it."

"But I haven't raised any questions yet. She couldn't possibly know that I'm planning to write about Ian's work."

"Unless he mentioned it to her."

Janet thought that, if Ian had told her about what Carol had decided, it implied an intimacy that went beyond the concerns of two scientists working side by side.

Carol frowned, disliking the implication. "No," she said. "Ian couldn't have told her anything. Why, the two of us have hardly had time to discuss it. Anyhow, he wouldn't . . . he wouldn't . . ." She stumbled and blushed.

But Janet understood. He wouldn't be talking to another woman about what concerned them so intimately. He had no such closeness with any other woman.

"He wouldn't," Carol said firmly. "I know he wouldn't."

Janet was inclined to agree. The obvious fury of the Chinese woman went beyond scientific opprobrium—even for a zealot. Anyone seeing Carol and Ian together in the lab would have recognized the tension between them. And, with very little effort, any Chinese in Beijing could have discovered that the two of them visited each other's rooms. That attack was by a jealous woman, if Janet was any judge. Had Ian Chen given her reason to believe that she was more to him than a colleague before Carol came along?

"Do you think she could have felt the same about Mary?" Carol startled Janet with the idea, as if the two of them had been following the same thought without speaking. They stared at each other.

Then Janet shook her head. "No, I don't think so. It seems to be common knowledge that Ian and Mary were just good friends."

"But maybe she felt that Ian's work—and China—were in danger from Mary. She seemed pretty excitable. She could be the one who . . . who . . ." The scene in Mary's room must have flashed before her eyes, because the blood drained from her face.

"It's not likely," Janet said quickly, hoping that her matter-of-fact tone would keep the awful scene away. "She's Chinese. How would she ever get past the guards at the hotel without being announced?"

"Hm-m. Unless she was such a frequent visitor that they let her through without question."

Carol frowned. She didn't like the idea at all.

"After all," Janet reasoned, "you and Ian haven't known each other very long."

"Of course." She sighed deeply. "I'm being silly. But somehow I can't imagine his being interested in someone so obviously unstable. He's such a rock himself—so sane, so together."

Janet bit her lip, suppressing the obvious remark. She was not a cynic, but she had no illusions about the attraction between men and women. She had seen the most levelheaded men completely besotted with airheads. And women too, of course. Anyhow, that was irrelevant. The real question was, who could have gotten into Mary's room without being seen and out again wearing bloody clothing?

"There are people here who don't trust Ian," Carol said. She was remembering the attack on him in the restaurant.

"Yes. You can't encourage a policy of wariness against foreigners and at the same time expect everyone to appreciate foreigners without reservations. It's schizophrenic policy and I'm sure it must drive some people crazy."

"That man believed Ian was a fake. He accused him of delaying final results in the tests—putting off doing field tests that he knew would work."

"I suppose that very careful scientists do often frustrate those who are impatient to put science to practical uses. I imagine that Ian, with his concern for life, would be very sure of his results before he tested an unknown substance on people."

"But no Chinese who is not a worker on the compound could get through the gate without being stopped. That man at the restaurant couldn't have."

"They couldn't if you believe in the absolute infallibility of the P.L.A." Janet grinned. Of course. Some of her best good sense came out when she talked instead of just ruminating to herself. "We'd never believe that security guards in our own countries were that conscientious at their jobs. Why are we so willing to believe it of the Chinese?"

It was true: foreigners in China were so overwhelmed by the *idea* of China's form of government that they almost bought the belief in an omnipotent and omnipresent Big Brother. Actually the Chinese were no more efficient than the bureaucrats in any Western country. Janet thought of how billions of tax dollars could not provide trash-free city streets or effective schools. Chinese soldiers guarding a residential gate might very well get careless after four or five hours.

"But," she continued the argument aloud, "he'd never get out unnoticed with his clothes all bloody."

"Unless someone in the hotel helped him get a change of clothes," Dorothy suggested.

"There is no way that could be kept a secret. If it happened that way it won't be long before the officer discovers who helped him."

"Somehow I can't believe a woman was murdered so horribly over a birth control program."

When Dorothy put it that way, so baldly, it did sound faintly ridiculous. All that fury and blood over a government science project. Then a vision of bombed-out abortion clinics in the United States challenged Dorothy's doubt.

"You think there must have been a more personal reason?" Janet asked her.

"Well," she answered a little defensively, "they're always saying *'Cherchez la femme.'* Maybe it's time we tried *cherchez*-ing the man."

"Who? Husband? Lover?"

"Yes," Dorothy said complacently, as if she had solved the murder.

"Mark was terribly upset when he saw what had happened." Carol's mouth trembled. "He couldn't have been pretending."

"I wonder," Janet mused, "if he kept a change of clothes in Mary's room."

"Wasn't he staying with her?"

"I don't think so." Janet remembered what the officer had told her. Mark had not gone into the room with Mary after their evening together. He had left her . . . and she had been murdered.

"He could come and go as often as he pleased. He'd never be stopped at the gate. They don't worry about Westerners killing each other."

"Mary and Mark loved each other," Carol protested. "They had a very good marriage."

There it was again—that insistence on idealizing everything about Mary. Janet remembered Mark's look at dinner when Mary had patted his hand and said sweetly, "Mark is happy with the arrangement we have. He has all the advantages of marriage and no wife to keep tripping over."

"And Mary," Mark had answered through lips gone suddenly stiff, "Mary is just as happy. Who knows what she gets up to on her travels alone?"

It all sounded very good-humored, but there was a sharp edge to the words and the look that passed between them. Was the clue to Mary's murder to be found somewhere in that marriage?

"Whatever they had," Dorothy grinned, "it was certainly different. Mark wasn't your run-of-the-mill, middle-class husband."

"What do you know about him?" Carol demanded. "You've never even met Mark. You're just tossing suspicion around onto everyone. What about Ian? Maybe *he* killed Mary. Or maybe *I* did it. Do you think *I* could have done such a thing?"

"No, of course not," Dorothy said meekly. For once she refrained from turning a feeling into a joke. Carol's outburst was so intense, it embarrassed her.

"Carol," Janet soothed her, "it could have been any one of a billion people. Mary was no shy violet in this country. She was a very controversial figure."

But Dorothy didn't recant her feeling that the impetus for the crime was a very personal one. Dorothy might be cynical and funny, but she was also shrewdly perceptive. That, Janet thought, was what made her so cynical.

And that, she mocked herself, betrays your own cynicism.

Fifteen

"IT WAS NO USE, JANET. I just couldn't stop my head from spinning. It was awful."

Carol sat huddled in the easy chair in Janet's room telling her about the weekend finale. Again she had wakened Janet at 6 A.M. Didn't the child ever sleep?

"In spite of what you said at lunch yesterday, I kept going round and round with the names of the suspects we ticked off and discarded. Only Ian and I were left, and I know *I* didn't kill Mary."

Discarded suspects? Janet thought. They hadn't discarded many. What in the world was she talking about?

Carol went on about how she had paced her room when they got back from Bei Hai Park, giving way to vague fears she couldn't pin down. A knock on her door made her heart lurch, as if she was as afraid of the news from the outside as she was of the whirling mists in her head.

"What's the matter?" Ian asked her when she opened the door and stood there staring at him. "I didn't have to go home after all. The crisis fizzled out. Aren't you going to ask me in?"

She was unable to move away from the door. Suddenly concerned about her pallor and fixed eyes, he pushed gently past her, took her slack fingers from the doorknob and closed the door.

"What's wrong, honey?" As if she had never slammed out of his apartment—out of his bed—in anger. His arm around her shoulders guided her to the chair and she sank into it as if she had no will of her own. He knelt in front of her and held her. "Can't you tell me what's the matter?"

How could she put into words the nameless horror she was feeling? In the short time since they had met, he had become her whole life. How could she admit even to herself that he might have killed Mary Allen?

Janet started to protest that she had never suggested such a thing—that there was no evidence that Ian was involved, but Carol ignored that.

"All this has been too much for you." He tried to comfort her. "I know what you need," he said. He almost lifted her bodily from the chair, snatched her purse and a sweater that lay on the table nearby and moved her toward the door.

Downstairs at the car, for a moment she resisted getting in, but the pressure on her back almost forced her to bend into the front seat.

"Now relax," he said, "and let me do the driving." His sidelong grin brought no response. She felt numb, bombarded by contrary doubts and fears. It was as if her body was a battlefield and she was powerless to do anything but wait until the war was over.

He drove quietly for a while, making his way carefully through the bicycles and the occasional bus.

"Where are we going?" she was finally able to ask him. They had been on the road for almost half an hour and she was becoming more aware of their surroundings. They were coming to the outskirts of the city and traffic had almost disappeared. Traveling west, they were nearing the Western Hills, Xi Shan, and she could begin to make out the sparse shrubbery on the hillsides and staircases cut into some of them. "No climbing hills today, please," she implored. "I'm just not up to it. You'd have to carry me to the top."

"No, thanks," he answered in mock horror.

She made an enormous effort and tried to match his kidding tone. "Are you implying that I'm too heavy?"

He looked away from the road for a long moment and deliberately eyed her. "You," he breathed, "are not 'too' anything." He leered at her and got a weak smile in response.

"You were ready to leave!" she blurted out. "You act as if you don't care what happened!"

"I care, Carol. Mary was a friend. But I thought I had to go. My staff wired me there was a possibility we had a breakthrough and it was important to the whole program that I check it out immediately. But it turns out they overreacted. I was hoping that when I got back from California we would have something to celebrate. This trip was supposed to be a celebration."

"I was there, Ian! I saw it!"

"I know that now, and I'm sorry I wasn't there with you. But no one told me you found her. And there was nothing I could do."

She thought he sounded so cold, so unfeeling. He was not the compassionate man she had been so attracted to.

"Where are you taking me, Ian?"

"It's a special place." He smiled. "I've been thinking about it for some time."

"You sound as if we won't be getting back for a long while." Suddenly she didn't want to be here, alone with him.

"Maybe we won't. I'll leave it up to you."

"I can't miss my classes tomorrow. We'll have to be back in time for them."

"Don't worry, I've arranged everything. No one will miss you if we decide to stay."

"I don't want to go anywhere, Ian. I'm afraid. I mean, I'm tired. I really don't feel well."

"You'll feel better after a while, you'll see. It's a beautiful day and we're going to forget everything that's happened." He was smiling but there was something about the tone of his voice that brooked no denial. She was being taken on a trip whether or not she wanted to go.

Her heart sank but she tried to settle back and relax. If she insisted on going back there might be an ugly fight and she was afraid of the consequences. Afraid. And he had arranged it so no one would miss her, try to find her. She felt sick.

After another hour's drive he pulled over to the side of the road.

They were surrounded, as far as the eye could see, by lush farm-lands. Here and there tiny blue and white figures worked in the fields, bent over the green or carrying buckets hanging from the ends of shoulder poles.

Neither one of them had said a single word during the hour. She had sunk into a sort of hopeless apathy and she could barely get up the energy to ask the question. "Why are we stopping here?" There wasn't a soul nearby.

"Think of this stop as a decompression chamber. From here we go back several thousand years, to the way my ancestors lived." He spoke lightly but there was a strong undercurrent of emotion in his voice and he looked at her intently to see her reaction.

She had a quick flash of the Ming Tombs, echoing vaults for the dead. Ancient tombs were often built in the countryside, where propitious winds could reach them and unwanted visitors could be seen for miles and turned back.

"Some people think," he went on, "that the revolution brought everyone in China into the twentieth century, but it didn't."

"Aren't these farms all collectivized?" she managed to ask.

"They tried, but it never really worked. Now they've instituted the Responsibility System. But all those decrees and orders go on in Beijing. Here, revolution or responsibility, it's all the same to the peasants. They tend the land the way their ancestors did and put their faith in tradition and the strength of the family."

She was intrigued in spite of herself. "Do you have relatives here?"

"Yes. I'm taking you to them. My father's uncle, his sons and their wives, his grandchildren and *their* wives and children."

"They all live together?"

"More or less. The land is held and worked in common. Houses are built as they're needed. No one has left the area since my father decided to go to America and pick some gold from the hills of California."

"Is this your first visit since coming to China?"

"Yes. I've written to say I'd be coming but I haven't had the chance until now."

"They won't be expecting a stranger—me."

"Don't worry. They'll welcome you, I'm sure."

But she was worried. She felt very uncomfortable about meeting his family, almost as if she were a prospective bride being taken to be presented to the patriarch for his approval. Or a prospective victim being shepherded into the hinterlands, away from her friends, from anyone who spoke her language.

She shivered. The sun was shining. It was a perfectly ordinary day and Ian was suggesting a day in the country. She must be losing her mind. Or, at least, her sense of perspective. The very normalcy of the day was oppressive. It must be the awful smell of human ordure that was wafted off the fields on the gentle breeze.

"Oh, come on, don't look like that! How many foreigners have the opportunity to stay in a peasant's house and live like one of the family? It will be an experience you'll never forget!"

She smiled wanly. He started the car and took off again, certain that he had convinced her, or carefully ignoring the fact that he certainly had not.

In another fifteen minutes they came to a village. It was only a collection of small buildings, some made of mud brick, one or two of the larger ones built of wood. Several of them were arranged around a square and were obviously shops. One of the wooden ones looked like a sort of town hall, with its bell tower and its row of old men sitting out front. It might have been the town hall in any rural American town, except that the old men all had brightly colored birds in wooden cages that they periodically swung to and fro, gently compelling each small occupant to fly from one perch to another in order to maintain its equilibrium.

Ian caught her staring and he explained. "They're exercising their pets. The value of such a pet was determined in antiquity. Many old men keep the tradition alive."

"Sad," she murmured, still feeling anxious and still trying not to.

"The men are very proud of their pets. And they're not lonely or unhappy. They have their families, and they know they've fulfilled the destiny of a man—working hard, preserving the land, rearing sons."

"And daughters?"

He grinned. "Daughters, too, of course. But first always, sons."

"Hmf." She sniffed at his teasing, resenting the complacency in it. "Is your uncle one of the men sitting there?"

"I don't know. I've never seen him." He pulled up near the front of the building and went to ask for directions to the house of Chen.

She looked around half hoping to see someone who might understand her, someone from whom she could get a ride back to the city. But she knew there wasn't much chance of that. She was beginning to resign herself to whatever happened.

He came back laughing. "Everyone seems to be Chen in this village, but they know my uncle. He's an important man hereabouts."

She gazed around at the few modest buildings and the wide expanse of emptiness immediately surrounding them. She sometimes thought it would be comfortable to live in a small pond—and aspire to be a big fish in it. Being able to literally touch the limits of one's world might take a lot of the anxiety out of living.

"Wouldn't it be easy to stay here forever? No conflicts, the answers all written large for you in history and tradition. It would be so *comfortable.*"

Perversely she denied the attraction. "I've never felt safe in the country."

He seemed startled for a moment, but he recovered quickly and leaned into the car. "Don't be afraid," he said seriously. "I'll protect you."

She looked at him closely, hoping for a clue to his real motive in bringing her here. He avoided her eyes, a small frown wrinkling his forehead.

But, seated behind the wheel again, he seemed determined to keep the mood light. "To Uncle's house we go," he sang, his strong baritone ringing back to the surprised old men. How could he sound so happy when she was feeling so down? she thought. He couldn't be the man for her if he was so insensitive to her feelings.

Ian's father's uncle was a wizened little old man who was delighted to see his grandnephew. But no more delighted than the cousins and their wives and what seemed like an army of children of all ages. "We Chinese don't believe in population control," he told her, straight-faced.

They all gathered around at first, talking at once. Then tea was brought, and cakes, and they sat and talked, with Ian translating sporadically for Carol. She didn't mind that she couldn't understand most of what was said. The open good will, the laughing sidelong looks at her, the antics of the smaller children all entertained and warmed her, until she almost forgot her fears and doubts. She felt like one of the family, welcomed, even cherished as someone who was needed to complete the charmed circle. She smiled, nodded, nibbled at the cakes and cooed at the babies. In a little while one of the three-year-olds was sitting on her lap, another leaning against her legs. There was no sense of strangeness at all.

Ian said something and everyone seemed to be expressing good-natured surprise and amusement.

"What did you say?" she asked him.

"I said we'd like to help a little in the fields. Have you ever had the urge to put your hands in the dirt, touch growing plants, pick fruits and vegetables ready for eating?"

She nodded. She had felt like that, but the closest she had ever come to it was watering a passion plant in a twelve-inch pot and pinching off an occasional browning leaf. Even that plant was only a memory now; there was no room for plants or pets in the life of someone who needed to take off as the impulse moved her.

At a word from the old man everyone got up. Apparently a decision had been made. Carol looked at the smiling, healthy faces of the children. Unheard in the small roar of good spirits, Ian murmured to her, "Here's the other side of the argument. A family filled with joy, all working together to help feed themselves and the nation. But more than that: they fulfill a millennia-old tradition. Strength in the family. Strength *through* the family. This is China's heart."

She could see pain in his eyes and in the tight lines around his mouth. How well he presented himself as the picture of the self-confident scientist, and how conflicted he was about his work. He had admired her when she recognized that he used Mary as his alter ego, encouraged her to argue the case against him. But how long could anyone keep going when he was struggling with such enormous contradictions? Maybe he had had enough—and had silenced that alter ego.

"I think that if the government ever succeeds in convincing the peasants of China that they should limit their families to a single child it will destroy the heart and soul of the country. What will be left will farm the land with technological skill but with no joy. And the old men you saw in front of the town hall will sit there just waiting to die. They won't be honored patriarchs; they'll be over-the-hill agricultural engineers forced to retire because the company's efficiency expert says they can't pull their own weight anymore, and the bottom line demands that they be gotten rid of."

Why had Ian Chen come to China? Because he respected the Chinese struggle to improve their material lot through population control and he wanted to help? Or did he want to get in touch with his roots in the land of his fathers? The man who accused him of faking his research; his support of Mary Allen; the respect that Dr. Hu Jiang and the students had for him—where did the truth about this man lie?

"Are all families as successful as the ones here?" she asked.

"No, that's part of the problem. If the population continues to grow at the same rate, people will go hungry. And as industry expands, there will be even less food. There is no simple solution."

The family caught them up in the laughing and joking and moved them toward the door.

"Where are we going?"

"They're taking us to a place where we can change our clothes. What you're wearing is not exactly what the well-dressed peasant needs for mucking about in the . . . uh . . . muck."

She looked down at her pristine white sandals and the elegant lavender dress. Its sleek skirt hugged her hips, and she couldn't help laughing. "I can just see myself squatting over a row of cabbages in this. The knife-edge crease in your pants won't last very long either. But what will we change into?"

"You'll see," he said. "The latest design by Dior for rice paddies and soybean fields."

One of the young wives handed each one of them a bundle of clothes and a straw hat, and the whole crowd, including the smallest child, was pushing and urging them out of the house and down the road. Only the old man remained behind, calmly smoking his long-stemmed pipe and nodding with satisfaction at the new additions to his family. Although he no longer worked in the fields there was nothing over-the-hill about *him*. He presided over all family discussions, nodding his approval or letting his experience and knowledge lead the ones he loved away from dangerous or unproductive paths. While his wife lived, her wisdom had strongly influenced him, although she had made her wishes known in the privacy of their bed. Now his children and grandchildren and great-grandchildren looked to him with sincere respect and affection to provide solidity and continuity to their lives. Carol, a stranger to this place and this culture, felt the sense of security and peace here, and a part of her envied them all.

Janet snorted skeptically. Though she recognized the pull of the child in Carol toward a life ruled by an omnipotent grandfather, she was quite sure that her friend would feel stifled in such an environment. She hoped that Carol was not contemplating submitting to such an illusion of security. Was Ian Chen one of those men who wanted to dominate his family, rule like the old patriarchs?

Carol went on with her account, more as if she were talking to herself than to Janet. As the afternoon went on, she had obviously become more and more enthralled with the family, the farm and even Ian.

It was different in the countryside than in the city. There, when there was insufficient living space, it was relatively easy to carve another room out of the hillside or put up a mud hut at the side of a field. Whole families were not forced to live in one room while waiting for cement apartment blocks to go up. There was even room for guests, and Carol and Ian were shown to a house of their own—not luxurious, but clean and dry. When they were settled in they agreed that it was even cozy.

There was a small table and two chairs in the one-room house, and in the corner opposite the bed a wood-burning cook stove. A boxlike structure provided the base for the bed. On it was a thin pallet over which snapping clean sheets were spread, and a brocade quilt sewn into a cotton cover, with the center left exposed for beauty. Over the two pillows with cotton slips were terry-cloth hand towels. No one seemed to know exactly what this was for; perhaps to keep the hair from staining the pillow slips. Apparently their hosts expected them to sleep together. This meant they thought they were married; the Chinese did not condone pre- or extramarital sex.

As a matter of fact, Janet thought, they behaved as if sex were nonexistent.

Carol stared at the bed after everyone had left and heard herself saying, "We've come to no decision about this. We must talk about it." Marriage here was a statement made to family and community that a man and a woman were now part of that family, to be recognized by that community as a new family unit. There was no way to be casual about accepting the hospitality of the senior Chen and his offspring.

At the same time she was surprised that she could even think about marriage when murder was still on her mind. She didn't want to be alone in this house with Ian, far from a telephone or the sound of someone else's voice.

"Not now, Carol," he broke gently into her thoughts. "Look, change your clothes and come out to the fields with me. Let's just enjoy the rest of the day and let the future take care of itself. I'll wait until you're dressed, then I'll change."

She bit her lip and sighed. *Why* did everything have to be so complicated? Why was she so suspicious—so scared?

Slowly she shed her Western dress and put on the baggy blue cotton pants and white shirt. There were even white socks and cloth shoes in the bundle, and the large straw hat would protect her from the sun. With her red hair hidden and her eyes shadowed by the hat, and with her darkly tanned skin, she must look

like the other women in the village. She knew it was true when
she saw the look on Ian's face. "Two hundred years of modernization stripped away," he murmured. "Who said clothes don't make
the woman?"

She had the same reaction when she saw him changed—a Chinese peasant, a rather tall one. Almost she expected that he would
speak Chinese to her—and that she would understand it.

Together they walked toward one of the men standing in the
middle of a field waving to them. Smilingly he illustrated what
they were to do—pull the small, grasslike weeds from the rows of
large green plants. Cabbage, she thought. At short distances
around them others were bending over the rows, absorbed in the
work, although she could hear the talk and the laughter, probably
about them.

City people though they were, they bent to the job, moving
along the row. After a while Carol groaned as she straightened up.
"Is there something else we can do for a while, so I can learn to
walk upright again?"

"Oh-h-h, that's a good idea. Maybe we can carry water. That
should equalize the pain a little."

The older man at the well—a cousin—fixed the pole across Ian's
shoulders and hung a bucket of water from each end. He turned
too quickly, almost knocking Carol over with one of the buckets,
and staggered upfield where his cousin pointed. Carol preferred to
carry a bucket the usual way, and she followed him, laughing as
she watched his buckets swing wildly with every step as he
fought to keep his balance.

At nightfall they stood in the field looking at each other and
burst out laughing. They were covered in mud from toes to knees,
with half the field under their fingernails. He brushed her face to
remove a large smudge of mud and only smeared it more. They
were both exhausted.

"Can you make it back to the house?" he asked.

"No, I think I'll just lie down here and go to sleep."

"I'd like to join you, but I prefer joining you in bed."

She looked quickly around at the other blue and white figures
who had also finished work and were drawing closer to where

they stood. For a moment she thought they had heard and understood.

"Would you like me to repeat it in Chinese?" he asked soberly.

She decided to go him one better and shake him up. *"Wo ye yao qu chuang,"* she said clearly so that the people nearest to them must have heard her. She was gratified to see his jaw drop before he grabbed her arm and ran with her out of the field and onto the road that led to their temporary home.

"You devil!" he laughed. "You want to shock the socks off these good people?"

"You think they understood me?" she laughed, breathless from running.

"I hope not. Your Chinese is awful."

"Hah! Then why are you blushing?"

"Wives just don't say to their husbands that they want to go to bed."

She came to an abrupt halt in spite of the strength in his arm. "Wives?"

His white teeth shone through the tan and dirt. "All I said was that we were staying the night. They assumed the rest."

"Oh, assumed. And you couldn't say anything to set them straight, could you?"

"They'd make me share Cousin Li's bed and put his wife in with her daughter! You wouldn't want to cause all that unhappiness, would you?"

"I would," she said, quite definite, and she resumed the walk to the house.

They took turns at the outdoor shower, each carefully arranging to dress while the other was engaged elsewhere. Under other circumstances it could have been a tantalizing delaying tactic, when all roads led to *chuang.*

Then there was a banquet to attend, this time down to beer instead of maitai. And by nine-thirty everyone was ready for bed. Carol and Ian were ushered ceremoniously to their house. They stopped inside the door, listening to the family make their cheerful way to their own houses, and a heavy, fragrant silence descended on the world. The touch of his hand moving feather-light on her back seemed a part of the silence.

She felt her back stiffen and the fear came again. "Let's go back to Beijing," she said breathlessly.

"Now?"

"Yes. Right now. I want to go back right now."

"Aw, have a heart, Carol. I'm tired."

She looked at him almost with hostility, though it was a rising panic that kept her silent. She saw the anger come slowly to his face, the way his mouth and jaw tightened.

"Okay, if that's what you want. I'll just leave a message in the main house." He turned abruptly and left, and she breathed a sigh of relief.

In a few minutes he was back again, and they were on the way back to the city. He was furious, and said not a word to her until they were almost home.

"I don't know what you've got on your mind. I don't understand you. I thought I did. I was wrong about you."

"And Mary?" she almost screamed at him. "Were you wrong about Mary too?" Suddenly all the anxiety, all the tension, all the unanswered questions broke the dam holding back her frustration and anger. "I suppose that's all you were to each other—just good friends! Tell me, when did you decide that she wanted to be more than a friend?"

"What the hell are you talking about?" he yelled back, and jerked the car over to the side of the road.

"No! Don't stop driving! I don't want to sit here in the dark with you!"

A great quiet fell between them, and he looked at her in amazement. "You're afraid of me," he said slowly. "I don't believe it. You're really afraid of me."

"Th-that's ridiculous! I'm not afraid of you or anyone else."

"You think I killed Mary."

"N-no." Her protest convinced neither one of them.

"She was my friend," he insisted.

"Sh-she could have destroyed your work."

"No. She did what she had to do and I respected her."

"She was more than a friend to you."

He frowned in exasperation. "Make up your mind, Carol. Which is it? Was she my lover or a threat to my work? Did she want to be my lover or did she want to destroy me? You're not making sense, you know."

There was no justifying her feeling, she thought miserably. It was just there. She huddled against the car door, unable to look at him. He sat for a few minutes, silently, then started the car and drove back to the Friendship Hotel. In front of her building he leaned across to open the door on her side and sat looking straight ahead until she got out. She stood uncertainly for a moment, then turned and went up the steps.

Sixteen

WHEN CAROL FINISHED telling Janet about the aborted trip to the countryside, she left for work. Anyone seeing her so perfectly turned out, so obviously in command of her appearance, her work, her life, would never have credited the fearful assessments that filled Janet's head. She wondered what Ian Chen thought about his experience. He was a competent physician; what would he say about the mood swings, the rapid mind changes, the fears he had observed in Carol?

Or—maybe I'm barking up the wrong tree, she thought. The paranoiac sounds crazy unless it's established that someone really *is* chasing him. *Had* Ian Chen's behavior been subtly menacing? Was Carol just sensitive enough to pick up cues that put her in fear of her life?

She shook off her own confusion and prepared to get dressed. Suddenly everyone looked crazy to her. It was not difficult to get into such a mind set; it had been demonstrated again and again that mental health professionals thought everyone they met professionally was crazy. It was a short step to thinking that everyone living in this strange world was somewhat off center.

She said something of the sort to the P.L.A. officer when they met after breakfast. He was coming from the clinic where Mark still lay in bed—grieving, apathetic, unwilling to get up.

"Most people are out of their element here, their real lives waiting to be taken up again when they go home. It's an unsettling way to live; it makes them behave oddly."

He nodded. "So it is difficult to recognize the character of someone who could have murdered Mrs. Allen. You did this very skillfully when Mrs. Li was murdered."

"At that time I knew all the people involved so much better."

"You did not know Mrs. Allen well?"

"No. I met her several days ago, the same time Carol Walker did. And I've known Carol only since I arrived in China about a week ago. I've talked to Mark only once."

"All of you have met only recently and yet Miss Walker seems so disturbed by what has happened."

"I feel so sorry for Carol. She'll need time to get over this."

"Do you think Miss Walker had anything to do with the crime?"

"What? Certainly not!"

"She suffers as with the loss of someone very close. One might believe that they knew each other well," he said quietly, looking at her intently. Did he recognize the worrying doubts that masked her too quick denial?

"They just met and they liked each other." She crossed her fingers. No point in bringing up the initial hostility Carol had shown toward Mary. No wonder policemen were universally suspicious of "civilians." Even those who didn't lie to them rarely told them the whole truth. "They were planning a series of articles for scientific journals in the U.S."

"The kinds of articles we have come to expect from Mrs. Allen?"

Janet shook her head, almost as if she were disclaiming responsibility.

"A curious project for someone who was in love with Dr. Chen."

"What do you mean? Dr. Chen and Mrs. Allen managed to stay very good friends."

"Yes," he said thoughtfully. "Perhaps you can help me to understand that friendship. It seems to me that Mrs. Allen was concerned to stop Dr. Chen's work. She thought what he was doing was immoral."

"She did, but I think, with someone like Ian Chen, the usual criteria can't apply. He respected Mrs. Allen and her work. He wants the world to find other ways of surviving."

"Curious. I have talked with Dr. Chen about this. Perhaps we can discuss it again."

She smiled sympathetically. He was stuck with a bag of foreign suspects, when solving a murder required discernment and understanding of motives. Difficult enough with people in one's own culture.

"How is Mark Allen feeling?" she asked him.

"He is calm now, but very unhappy. It will take time for him to recover. It was a shock to come on the scene—to lose his wife. We will not disturb him yet."

She nodded. "A dreadful experience for him." They continued their walk silently for a moment before she asked, "He didn't spend the night in his wife's room?"

"No."

"Does he give a reason?"

"He refuses to say where he was. Did he not come to Beijing to be with his wife?"

"That's what I assumed. Maybe they had an argument and he went to spend the night with a friend."

"Why should he refuse to say?"

She grinned. "Maybe it was another woman."

"A foreign woman or Chinese?"

"I have no idea." She was reluctant to point out that he might be protecting the identity of a Chinese woman who would be in real trouble if it was discovered that she was sleeping with a foreigner. Or, for that matter, sleeping with any man without benefit of marriage. Not clergy, of course. Most Chinese had long ago stopped being concerned about benefit of clergy. She refused to think about the possibility that he had been with a man; that might lead them up a blind alley cluttered with prejudices.

Maybe she should tell him that Dorothy's John Peter knew Mark. Was it Dorothy Parker who had urged her love in a foreign land not to lie alone at night—that she would understand? If Mary had said the same thing to her love, the fact that Mark had lovers was not relevant to the murder of his wife. Even if the lovers were men. She hated to think she would be relaying this information only because homosexuality was still so often food for salacious gossip.

She decided to say nothing about it.

"The worker at the desk says he saw Mr. Allen come out earlier. About the time his wife may have been murdered."

"He did? I can't believe it! It must have been before Mary was murdered."

"Six o'clock, he says."

"How did he look?" She remembered the scream of anguish that tore from his throat when the P.L.A. man let him into Mary's room. He couldn't have seen it earlier and faked his collapse.

The officer shook his head impatiently. "I hear that in the West people think Chinese are—what is the word?—inscrutable. Here too there is such a problem. But we, perhaps, have a better reason for such foolishness. The young man behind the desk comes recently from a small town. He has seen very few Westerners. It is almost impossible for him to recognize feelings in Western faces. He can say only that Mr. Allen was not smiling when he left. He did not stop; only walked from the hotel."

"Was he hurrying? Did he walk quickly?"

He shrugged. "Just walked. He saw nothing more."

"He wasn't registered in the hotel."

"No," he said. Then, surprisingly, "He came to Beijing a week before the murder."

"Are you sure? Mary said—or implied—that he didn't arrive until the day we all had dinner together."

"That is one thing we have been able to determine very easily. His visa was checked at the airport a week earlier."

"Did he have business here? I thought his only reason for coming to Beijing was to see his wife."

"He will not say. You did not see Mr. Allen go up to his wife's room after your evening together?"

"No. We dropped them at the hotel at about eleven. Then Dr. Chen drove me to my door."

"And Miss Walker?"

"I left them both sitting in the parked car."

"I will speak to Dr. Chen again."

"You really suspect Carol, don't you? Why?"

"Does her reaction to Mrs. Allen's death seem . . . er . . . uh . . . excessive to you?"

"No, I don't think so. Anyone coming on that bloody scene would have gone to pieces. Look at Mark."

"Yes, he grieves. But Miss Walker seems quite calm now. I spoke a few words with her this morning."

"Well, she could hardly be expected to grieve for as long as Mary's husband does. After all, they just met. Her reaction was more shock at the scene. Once that diminished, she recovered."

"Yes," he said thoughtfully. "Now she tells me that she and Dr. Chen were together all night."

"So? They're Americans," she pointed out.

He smiled faintly. "But only one of those Americans says they were together until six o'clock."

"You mean Ian Chen denies it?"

"He said this before I spoke to Miss Walker. We talked on the telephone. He says she left at about four-thirty."

She bit her lip. Damn!

They entered the lobby of the tourist hotel and he motioned Janet to the easy chairs. "Have you a thought about this?" he asked when they were settled.

"Hm-m. Not a very pleasant one. Was either of them seen going up to Mary's room?"

"We must question the worker at the desk more closely. For now, he volunteers only that Mark Allen went out in the morning."

John Peter came down the steps into the lobby and raised his hand in greeting as he passed. Behind him the desk man motioned excitedly to the officer, who excused himself and went to see what he wanted.

When he came back he almost threw himself into the chair with exasperation. She had never seen him give way to frustration like this.

"What did he want?"

"He tells me that the man came down the steps in the same way."

"The same way?"

"Yes. The one who just went out. He came down the steps the same way he did the morning of the murder."

"But I thought you said he identified Mark Allen—"

"Yes, yes." He motioned impatiently. "He says it is the man who stays with the foreign woman."

"Which foreign woman?"

"And which man? He cannot say which one is Mark Allen and which one is this John . . . John . . ."

Janet felt a surge of hysterical laughter. "You mean they all look alike to him?"

He tried to look fierce, not to laugh, as he sat watching her giggle uncontrollably.

Finally she was able to say, "But it must have been Mark Allen he saw." She checked her watch. "John sleeps late in the morning, Dorothy told me. He hates getting up before eleven. Not only that, but he's been having a hard time getting over his jet lag. At any rate, he'd have no reason for murdering Mary Allen. He had no connection with the Allens." She said it impulsively, and even as she heard herself saying the words she knew that she was probably wrong.

The officer confirmed what she had not yet clarified in her own mind. "This John Peter Brigham works in Tokyo. And Mrs. Allen's husband also lives in Tokyo. It is possible that there is a connection." He had certainly left no one uninvestigated.

"Tokyo is a big city," she argued perversely, wanting to hear solid reasons for pursuing this angle.

"Beijing is also a big city. Yet foreigners find their way to each other."

"Hm-m, maybe. There are so many more foreigners in Tokyo, and they've been coming and going there for so much longer."

"They are two men of an age, living alone in the city, both

speaking the same language. I do not think it is so . . . uh . . . farfetched? . . . that they meet and perhaps even know each other well."

"But," she pushed the argument, "what possible reason could John Peter have for killing Mark's wife?"

He gave no answer. Both of them knew that they could find a hundred reasons if they were going to sit and speculate about it. The permutations and combinations of human relationships were infinitely varied.

The noise of a motorcycle invaded the morning quiet and a frown creased Janet's forehead. "Stupid way to get around," she grumbled. She hated the sound of the damn thing. "There's another Westerner. Maybe the young man at the desk would like to identify him as the murderer."

"Ah, yes, the Algerian who rides the motor bicycle."

"Have you interrogated him yet?"

"A very angry man. The noise of the machine shouts his anger to the world."

"Why was he ever permitted to get one? Not only does it pollute the air with noise but it's a hazard on the road crowded with cyclists."

He shrugged. "He paid for it with French francs. China needs foreign currency."

She tightened her lips. Always people were at the mercy of abstract values. Governments sounded so certain about the importance of those values but economic depressions came and went with devastating regularity no matter how the politicians struggled to regulate the currency.

"He hated Mary Allen, I think. Perhaps, also, they were once lovers. He says that he tired of her. That he broke off their relationship. But somehow I doubt that. I think Mary began to be bored by his craziness. She was far too intelligent to stay with him for very long."

"You do not think he is intelligent?"

"Too much anger makes one stupid. He feels he was betrayed by the French government when it advocated that black Algerians be given the vote. And he sees Mary Allen's opposition to China's population control as the same kind of betrayal."

"That is very strange. Mrs. Allen had no power to change China's policy."

"I don't know if he felt that way before he met Mary—when he knew only her writing. Or if he began to feel that way after she broke up with him."

"You think he might have murdered her?"

"It's a possibility. Maybe he was the one the man at the desk saw."

But he definitely wasn't. When he was brought to confront him, the desk man was positive. No, no. This man he knew. He was the one who rode the noisy machine. He had lived on the compound for a long time. He was not the man who had gone up or come down either last night or this morning.

So, after all, all Westerners did not look alike to him.

"What was your impression of Mrs. Allen's character?" the officer asked Janet as they walked out of the lobby.

"I'd just met her, but she was an . . . er . . . impressive woman."

"Impressive? Ah, yes, I understand. Very strong woman. So very certain she was correct in her beliefs."

"The kind of woman who makes enemies. Have you considered that she was not murdered by a foreigner?"

He sighed. "Do you believe that I would not have considered that?"

"I'm sorry. I didn't mean that the way it sounded. It's just . . . there are so many people here who must resent what she wrote about China."

"There are not many who knew what she wrote. Perhaps some of those who worked closely with Dr. Chen."

"Do you know Dr. Hu Jiang? She works in the Beijing laboratory."

"Oh, yes. We see her often on the television. She is very well known in China. A famous scientist. You have met her?"

"When we visited the lab. She was very angry with Mary." Janet told him about the encounter. "But of course she would have been recognized if she had come to the gate. Has anyone mentioned seeing her?"

"She has been here often. You have not seen this on the television?"

She laughed. "I'm afraid I don't look at it very often." The endless scenes of government officials greeting other government officials and seating themselves ceremoniously on antimacassared chairs, while a rapid Chinese commentary in dulcet feminine voice presumably explained what was happening. She thought that even if she understood the language she would not be very interested. And there was no mistaking the elaborate ads for Chinese cigarettes. After a decade of not seeing them on American TV the exhortations to smoke sounded obscene, even when she didn't know exactly what the words were.

"Dr. Hu comes to the clinic to examine the foreigners—for swimming."

"Oh, yes." She knew that, before being permitted to use the pool on the compound, everyone was required to submit to a medical examination. Not a bad idea, of course, since they used no antibacterial agents to keep the water germ free.

"She is there now. We can speak with her."

Janet was inordinately pleased that he included her in the interrogation. This time she had no anxiety that he was trying to discover if *she* had done the murder.

Seventeen

"DR. HU IS VERY BUSY."

The director of the clinic was reluctant to let them take the doctor's time. The weather was still warm in the afternoons and many people were deciding that they wanted to swim. There were hundreds of examinations to make and Dr. Hu could give only two hours a day to the clinic.

When they finally got past the director, the doctor was more cooperative. Janet was surprised again at how infrequently the officer used the power of his authority. Here too he relied on persuasion and explanation to get what he could have got more easily by pushing.

Janet sat in a chair beside the desk in what looked like a doctor's office anywhere in America, except for the acupuncture charts on the walls: body diagrams with notations for the different pressure points. Through an open door she could see an examining room with a table and a hospital bed. Dr. Hu sat at the desk and the officer in a straight-backed chair facing her. It was more like a professional consultation than a police interrogation.

"How can I help you?" She spoke in English, probably out of deference to Janet.

"You were acquainted with Mary Allen?" the officer asked her.

"I knew of her. I spoke to her one time, in Dr. Chen's laboratory. But I did not know her."

There was no sign of the animosity she had expressed that day at the laboratory.

"You did not . . . uh . . . appreciate her views." It was a mild statement, almost teasing in tone. Janet wondered just how important Dr. Hu was. The officer was being more circumspect than she would have expected even from such a tolerant man.

"I did not. She did not count the cost."

"Perhaps she did. Perhaps her reasons were well thought out."

"I did not think so. From her writings, it was clear that she saw only what she wanted to see. She had no right to put our program in danger."

"There are many at the laboratory who agree with you?" he asked quietly.

"All agree with me. Except . . . except . . ." For the first time her poise showed a crack. Janet held her breath and waited for a name.

"Except Dr. Chen?" the officer asked. His voice was very low.

"He is a most unusual man," she said. Her jaw was stiff. She no longer looked like the cool professional in command of the situation.

"You spoke to Dr. Chen about Mrs. Allen?"

"I tried. He said *she* was the one to talk to . . ." She stopped abruptly. She hadn't wanted to say this.

"And did you take his advice? *Did* you go to her room to talk to her?"

"No."

They sat looking at each other. The doctor's mouth twitched convulsively once. The officer sat, completely at ease, waiting.

Finally, "I did not talk to her."

"You did not go to her room?" he asked ingenuously.

Her mouth twisted into a bitter half smile. "I did not *talk* to her." A pause. Then, "She was already dead."

He nodded. "You came into the room."

"Yes. I had to see if I could help her, but I knew it was useless." She sat back in her chair, her arms enfolding her body as if she was suddenly cold, her eyes staring down.

Janet remembered. The footprints across the floor. Small footprints. She sighed inaudibly. Not Carol's.

He didn't ask Dr. Hu why she hadn't reported what she had
found. He was probably right: what difference did it make what
she said? That she was afraid to incriminate herself? Reluctant to
get involved with the authorities? Wanted to postpone the questioning of her friends and colleagues—of Ian Chen?

"Did you hope that Dr. Chen would be able to leave before the
body was discovered?" he asked casually.

Her eyes snapped up at him. "You dare to suggest that Dr. Chen
would do such a thing!"

He didn't answer but they all knew that what he was suggesting was that *she* thought Ian might have been involved.

"The murder of this woman has nothing to do with us! We are
scientists. We study, we work. We do not kill."

"Hm. What time did you go to the room?"

"About seven o'clock in the morning."

How characteristic, Janet thought. The Chinese day started
when most Americans were just turning on their sides for forty
more winks.

"No one saw you come or go?"

"No. There was no one at the desk. Of course there were people
all about outside, passing."

"How did you know which room Mrs. Allen had? Had you
been there before?" Janet asked.

Her head jerked toward Janet. Maybe she had had more to do
with the murdered woman than she was admitting.

"N-no. Y-yes. I . . . I . . . ."

"When were you in that room before?" the officer demanded.

She pulled herself up visibly. "The explanation is simple. The
day before, I decided to speak to her. I came to the desk and asked
for the room number. When I went up there was no answer to my
knock so I went away. I remembered the number."

"The door was not locked the second time?"

"I knocked. There was no answer. She could not be out so early,
I thought. I wanted very much to speak to her. So I turned the
. . . uh . . . er . . . the knob. The door opened."

The only way to lock those doors—from either inside or outside —was with a key. The murderer would hardly have locked the door and taken the key with him.

As if he followed her thoughts, the officer murmured, "The key was in the door." Then, "You were dressed as you are now—in a white coat?"

"Yes. Afterward, there was a smear of blood on the sleeve, from when I bent to the body. But . . ." She shrugged. Who would notice a smear of blood on a doctor's coat?

He rose to end the interview and Janet got up too. Dr. Hu sat there watching them leave as if she had forgotten that she was still sitting. Janet noticed the scale just inside the door and felt a knee-jerk impulse to weigh herself, to see if the lard-laced cuisine of China was getting to her hips, but she remembered the scale was calibrated in kilograms and gave up. She hadn't yet tried to master the metric system. Probably never would get around to it.

"Dr. Chen is at the college today and we will meet for lunch here. Would you like to join us?"

"Yes, I would. I haven't seen him since our dinner together." The enthusiastic response sounded too social. What she hoped for was the opportunity to hear his idea of what had happened, his version of the trip to the country with Carol, his opinion of Dr. Hu and of the Allen marriage. If he was asked the right questions she might not have to be the one to tell the officer about all her vague impressions of contradiction, conflict and confusion.

Eighteen

WHEN IAN CHEN stepped out of the chauffeur-driven car in front of the dining room that served Western food he put out his hand to the officer. They shook hands with every appearance of friendship. The officer had not mentioned that they had known each other before this business, but she should have guessed when he had said something about getting information from Ian on the phone. A policeman does not interrogate strangers by telephone.

Ian and Janet also shook hands and the three of them went in.

"I'm glad you're here," Ian told Janet when they were seated. "You're Carol's friend. She trusts you."

That was an odd qualification of their relationship, Janet thought. It seemed to bring into focus her concern about Carol's emotional state.

"Is she all right?" she asked him. "Did you see her at the college?"

"I saw her. She seems . . . uh . . . calm . . ." His voice trailed away and he frowned.

She waited for him to say more, to indicate specifically what was worrying him about Carol. But he changed the subject abruptly. "I was hoping I'd have big news for the country," he said ruefully, directing the remark to the officer. "But it was a false alarm."

"You expected the problems of population control would be solved for China?"

"Well, maybe not all the problems, but my people in San Francisco thought they'd discovered something important, something that would have brought us very close. I'm afraid they were overreacting to the statistics of a small field study. Unfortunately, someone leaked it to the media. It may mean trouble for us."

"Why should a small error of enthusiasm interfere with further research? I can understand the disappointment of your staff and of our government here. But the work merely must continue, must it not?"

"That sounds so calmly logical but somehow it doesn't work just like that."

"There's no way of knowing," Janet observed, "how disappointment will affect reporters or the public or—especially—the politicians."

"Or even the academics who screen funding applications," added Ian.

"Do you believe there will be no money for your work in America?"

"That's possible." Ian shook his head. "They're getting more reluctant to provide funds for this kind of research. The antiabortion movement and other fundamentalist groups are very active. All scientific research is suffering. There's a general shortage of money for such things."

But never a shortage, Janet thought bitterly, for weapons of all kinds. "Surely," she said, "the Chinese government won't cut off funds for your research. There's no doubt that this is high priority for them."

"Yes, I'm not concerned about the work continuing here. That will go on until we've solved the big problems."

"Was not Mrs. Allen's writing a danger to your work? Might she not have influenced your government to discontinue its support?"

A look of pain crossed Ian's face. "I don't think so. I had hoped some sense of perspective would be the result. We wanted people to talk about the total problem, not just to tear at each other from both sides of the abortion issue."

Janet was honestly puzzled. "How would her writing do anything like that? All she did was harangue abortionists—called them murderers. Hardly a way to encourage dialogue."

"But she was well known in the media. And I know that basically she agreed with me. With time she would be permitted to soften her stance. You see, her editor . . ."

He saw the look on her face and stopped talking. How in the world could such a brilliant scientist be so gullible? Mary had sold him a bill of goods about her intentions. And while he had waited for her editor to come around and "permit" her to publish the whole story, she had free access to Ian and his work. He was probably also responsible for keeping the Chinese authorities from taking action against her, by convincing them that she was no threat and should be allowed to remain in China.

"My friend," the officer said gently, "Mrs. Allen was a woman of unswerving purpose."

"What do you mean? I know she believed in relieving the suffering of people. She wanted all the children of the world to be adequately fed and housed."

"I am certain she did. But I believe she also wanted your kind of work stopped."

Janet could see the scientist's jaw clamped. In chagrin at the growing realization that he'd been used? In anger that the officer was pointing out his foolishness? Or was it only stubbornness, because he had no intention of letting his friendship for Mary be sullied?

There was no point in persisting in this line of observation. The woman was dead and the job now was to find out who had killed her. It was possible that Ian's resistance to the idea that Mary had taken him in was only a pose. Maybe he had realized this earlier and, in a burst of anger at the betrayal of his trust, had killed her.

Or maybe she had recently wanted more from him and was somehow threatening him—his reputation, his work—if he wouldn't accede to her demands. She may have discovered the full extent of Mark's life in Tokyo and was planning to end the marriage. Perhaps she thought she had found an acceptable substitute in Ian, even though he was so much younger than she was. But Ian was apparently smitten with Carol. Had Mary threatened to announce that he had been delaying his work, that he had been cooperating with her to sabotage China's program? Threatened to expose him if he didn't drop Carol? Maybe she had even already started such a rumor, which might account for the attacks on him and Carol.

Janet shook herself a little, trying to throw off these thoughts. They were just wild fancy, she rebuked herself. There was no evidence of any of it. Unless, of course, one raised logical doubts that someone like Ian could be so dense. Or that someone like Mary had not known all along that Mark was gay.

"Do you think," Janet asked him, "that someone who objected to her views murdered her?"

"It's possible, I suppose. But actually there are very few people here who are familiar with her views. A few journalists and some of my staff in the laboratories here."

"Yes. Some of your staff. Carol told me about the man at the restaurant who accosted you. Was he one of the workers?"

"Probably. I don't know them all by sight."

"And I myself was witness to two attacks, both on Carol."

"Carol? What does she have to do with it?"

"Well, it happened after she had agreed to collaborate with Mary."

The officer broke in. "Miss Walker was attacked for her views of the program?"

Janet held up a cautionary hand. "I don't know that that was the reason. The verbal attack was in Chinese. But there was also a physical attack. It was only by chance that she wasn't badly hurt."

"Why was this not reported?"

"Afterward we weren't sure what had happened—or even if Carol was really the target. Anyway," she added as she saw the look on the officer's face, "I would have told you about it sooner or later."

"Who would know about their plan to collaborate? The morn-

ing that Mary was killed was the first time they were to get together to talk about it."

"We discussed it at tea the day of our visit to your lab. And
Carol says she went to Mary's room after tea. I think Mary made
the suggestion first when we were still in the laboratory. Just before Dr. Hu told Mary . . ."

"Dr. Hu? Surely you don't think Dr. Hu would kill!"

"All I'm saying is that she was very angry."

"Yes, she was angry. She believed that Mary was interfering
with our work."

"Was that the only reason for her hostility?"

Ian looked extremely uncomfortable. "Dr. Hu and I have been
. . . have been . . . She saw Mary as a . . ."

"As a rival for your affections?" Janet asked matter-of-factly.
There was just no polite or kind way to ask pertinent questions in
a murder investigation, she reminded herself.

Ian shrugged away his obvious embarrassment. He wasn't going
to say anything more about that.

"Do you think Mark might have been angry enough with his
wife to murder her?" she asked him.

He actually blushed. She remembered the way Mark had
looked at him the night of the dinner and she could understand
the blush. "The marriage was in trouble," he muttered.

"How well do you know Mark Allen?" asked the officer.

"I've known him as long as I've known Mary. He's very good in
his field—banking. A financial expert."

"And his personal life?"

Why was he asking? Janet wondered. Had he detected something in Mark's manner that would lead him to ask such a question?

"It must have been very difficult for him to live in Japan while
his wife lived in China," the officer went on. "Many of our young
married people are compelled to such an arrangement and it
presents difficulties."

Janet was surprised. The Chinese couples she knew seemed to
accept their separation rather stoically. Not that they weren't
often lonely and unhappy. She thought the officer was implying

that he was aware of serious problems—even police problems—among them.

Ian bit his lip. "I used to think it was a perfect marriage. But lately there was something . . ."

"He's gay," Janet interjected. "Did you know that?"

He looked at her, startled. "No. No, I . . . not exactly. . . . Just recently, in the last couple of visits, I thought I detected something . . . going wrong. . . ."

"I doubt that this was a recent thing. I wonder if Mary knew."

Ian shook his head. "She never said anything to me. Only talked about how satisfying her marriage was. She also talked about finding a way they could live together one day, without giving up their work. But she seemed content with the way things were."

"Yes, more content than Mark." How could Ian not have spotted the anger, the resentment? But he had surely been made uncomfortable by Mark's attraction to him, even though he couldn't admit it to himself.

"Mark would never have killed her. At worst, he could have asked for a divorce. What happened in that room was the result of white-hot rage. Mark's not like that."

Apparently the officer had given him a description of the scene of the murder.

"Maybe she was threatening to expose him. Even though homosexuality is more or less accepted these days, maybe an international financial expert needs to be like Caesar's wife." She cringed inwardly at the unintended pun, but neither of the men seemed to have noticed. Ian because he was worrying the idea of Mark as a murderer; the officer because he was probably unfamiliar with the reference.

"I can't imagine Mary blackmailing Mark."

No, Janet thought, you were her friend. You saw nothing devious or manipulative about her. But she was not a nice woman. And now there's Carol. What have you learned about Carol that's bothering you, that you're reluctant to admit to yourself?

Nineteen

THE THREE finished their lunch and left the dining room. The officer announced that he needed to question again some of the people in the hotel where Mary had had her room, and he left them. Ian and Janet strolled along the path of the compound. Suddenly, impulsively, Ian said, "If you're not busy, come to my apartment for a little while and have a drink. I'd like to talk to you about Carol."

She raised her eyebrows but went gladly. She wanted to know more about Carol from his point of view.

Up two flights of chipped concrete steps half lit by a low-watt bulb. From somewhere close by a baby wailed and a mother made soothing noises. Like the hotels, these apartment buildings on the compound also housed foreigners working in China. Usually they were families who needed cooking facilities. Janet preferred her living room and bedroom with bath, and people to clean and do her laundry.

They went through a dark, narrow foyer into a small room. Although it had started as a square space with two oblong windows cut into one of the walls, he had made something unique of it. The huge silk kite of red, blue, yellow and black in the shape of a moth covered one wall and set the color scheme for the other furnishings.

"Wherever did you find that chair?" She couldn't help exclaiming at the easy chair upholstered in black silk brocade shot through with red. The Chinese economy did not produce such elegant artifacts for domestic use.

He smiled. "It's the regulation plastic chair covered by a little upholsterer off Wangfujing."

She laughed at his teasing. Tourists were forever finding little tailors to make up traditional Chinese robes and jackets of the brocades they bought. "It's beautiful!"

"I bought the silk from him to send home to a friend. But then I thought it would look good right here. He said he could cover a chair and he came here and did it. Nice, isn't it?"

"It's a lovely room," she said. "Exotic, yet warm and comfortable."

He brought cool white wine in an exquisite china pitcher and delicate crystal glasses. "The rug is an ancient silk carpet. I saw it in one of those small theatrical costumers' that furnish stage settings for the Peking Opera. They didn't want to sell it, but I talked them into it." He stretched his long legs from the carved ebony armchair he was sitting in out to the low matching table between them. She had seen furniture like this in special tourist centers that required foreign currency for the purchase of all kinds of gorgeous things for shipment back to home countries—things that most Chinese people never saw.

She smiled and nodded as she looked about her, at the traditional rice paper paintings in black with touches of red, at the single three-foot-high blue vase in front of the windows where the light glancing off it reminded her of the fluted roofs of the Temple of Heaven. Even the books stacked on the floor along one pale green wall did not seem out of place. The bookcases in her own room were ugly, jerry-built affairs, and he had probably rejected what he had seen in the stores. Better no bookcase than a note of ugliness in this serene haven.

"I can't imagine a room like this in the States. It's so . . ."

"Chinese?"

"No," she said. "Or, at least, not modern Chinese. It looks like a remnant of one of the palaces I've seen, a part of a life I can hardly imagine. Yet there's nothing here that's all that different from contemporary furnishings. More beautiful than any I've ever seen, but the forms aren't so different."

"I feel as if I've drawn these things out of myself. I had to have them, to make contact with a part of myself. It all feeds my soul," he added, half kidding, half serious. "It's not easy being an overseas Chinese in China. It's not what I thought it would be." He quickly changed the subject. "See that small stone lion?"

"Yes. I've seen it somewhere before."

"It's one of the two hundred eighty lions that stand along the arches of Lugouqiao, the bridge Marco Polo described. That's one that cracked off during Chiang Kai Shek's march into Beijing. I'm sorry I won't be able to take it back with me if I return to the States. The ministry let me borrow it for the duration of my stay."

"*If* you return to the States?"

"*When* I return," he said firmly. "When I return."

He said nothing more, apparently not willing to reveal what seemed to be still another conflict going on inside him.

"I heard about your trip to the country to visit your family," Janet said tentatively. "Carol was delighted with the experience."

"Yes, it was good to see my family, to get some feeling for the life my father came from. They welcomed us."

"They welcomed Carol?"

"Yes. She was wonderful with them—especially the old man and the small children. She's a beautiful woman."

"You're very fond of her, aren't you?"

"Yes." He was lost in thought, and the quiet extended itself.

"Carol is very fond of you too," she told him.

"I know she is. But she's not a . . . a . . . a very happy woman, is she?"

"Happy? Maybe not . . . uh . . . unhappy." She waited for him to say more.

"She . . . confuses me. She keeps me guessing."

"Isn't that supposed to be the charm and mystery of a woman?"

He was right to gesture impatiently at the speciousness and artificiality of her teasing. She knew what he meant and it was nothing to joke about.

"No, there's something . . . something I don't understand about her. Something disturbing."

Janet said nothing, but her silence seemed to imply that she felt the same.

"Does Carol think I killed Mary?" he asked abruptly.

Janet gasped. "She never said anything about that to me."

"She actually seemed to be afraid of me—afraid I wanted to harm her in some way. Why would she feel like that about me?"

Janet shook her head. "I don't know. She has fears. She doesn't always explain very clearly."

"You didn't know her before you came here, did you?"

"Oh no. I met her here. She's from San Francisco. Isn't that where you're from too?"

"Yes, I . . ." He started to speak and then stopped.

She waited for him to go on, and when he didn't she asked, "You could have called on her family if you'd gone to San Francisco."

"Um . . . m. Odd you should think of that. Actually, I *have* talked to someone at San Francisco State University who knew her. She went to school there."

"Oh?"

"A scientist in my lab there said they thought very highly of her. She made a reputation for herself. They said she was brilliant. Brilliant and . . . and . . ."

"Erratic?"

"Yes. I suppose 'erratic' is a word, though it wasn't the one he used. 'Conflicted,' he said. 'Troubled.' She left there suddenly without saying why. She was almost finished with her Ph.D. thesis, but she just dropped it all."

There was a peremptory rapping on the door. Ian opened. "Carol!" He smiled, surprised and pleased.

She pushed past him and stopped abruptly to stare when she saw Janet seated there, the wineglass in her hand.

"Hi, Carol," Janet said.

As precipitously as she had pushed her way in, Carol turned and fled without a word. Ian and Janet looked at each other, mystified. Then Ian bolted out the door and down the stairs after her.

When Janet got up to look out the window she saw the two of them arguing on the path. Ian had a restraining hand on Carol's arm and she was struggling to free herself. Her face was stiff with anger and she had her head turned away from Ian, who seemed to be importuning her to calm down and listen to reason.

Just as suddenly as she had run from the apartment she now stopped all movement and stood absolutely still, her head down. Ian still held her arm, but he had stopped talking. Slowly he turned her around and walked with her back into the building.

Janet met them on the stairs. "I'll see you later," she said. Neither one of them answered. Except for her downcast eyes, Carol looked calm and as serenely beautiful as always, groomed to perfection. Her periwinkle-blue blouse made her hair look like live flame. No one seeing her in passing would have guessed at the turbulent storms that tossed her about and bewildered her friends.

Twenty

THAT AFTERNOON Dr. Hu was left lying on the path a hundred feet from the door of the clinic. She had been stabbed in the chest and she was unconscious but still breathing. The Algerian had almost run over her in the failing light but he had stopped in time when he saw the patch of white and got off his motorcycle to investigate. He explained this to the doctor on duty, who directed him to place Dr. Hu on one of the beds. She busied herself to help the unconscious woman. Before she could get around to summoning the police Armand disappeared, and she could hear the roar of the bike diminish in the distance.

Strolling back from dinner, Dorothy, John and Janet saw the army jeep with the huge red star on the side parked in front of the clinic. They stood desultorily discussing the possible reasons for the presence of the police.

"Maybe they're talking to Dr. Hu again," Janet suggested. "Her story seemed straightforward enough but policemen everywhere never are satisfied with a single telling. They seem to keep hoping that listening to accounts again and again will somehow reveal something significant they've been missing."

"You don't think that's true?" John asked her. "In fiction witnesses are always tripping themselves up and lies are exposed."

"In fiction," Janet laughed. "I think if witnesses change their stories it's not because they're remembering more accurately but because they're embellishing to make the story more interesting, or dropping salient facts because, on second thought, they don't seem important. From what we know about human perception, the eyewitness system needs some serious revision."

"Is Dr. Hu a suspect?" asked Dorothy. "She examined me for my swimming card. A pleasant woman."

"She was in the room—probably after Mary was murdered. She says she wanted to talk to her."

"How do you know it was *after* the murder?"

"Well, of course, that's what she says." Janet hadn't really thought much about it before but, as so often happened in her thinking, her ideas became clearer as she was speaking. "Her footprints," she said slowly. "They were all on top of the splashes of blood. As if she had walked in when the blood was almost dry. They led to the body and then away. No prints splattered. Even the few near the body that were smudged clearly lay over the spilled blood."

"You saw that?" Dorothy's voice was half horrified, half somewhat skeptical. "How long did you stay there to look around?"

"Not long, actually. But it's a scene that imprints itself on the brain. I had no idea that the details were so clearly up there." She tapped her head. "Until this minute."

"Then you're certain she couldn't have done it?"

She shrugged. "Maybe they've discovered something else—additional evidence. She could have murdered her and then come back later, to establish her innocence."

"But she didn't report finding the body," John pointed out. "It would have made no sense for her to come back and then sneak out again and hope no one would discover that she'd been there."

The officer came out of the clinic and, catching sight of them, approached. Janet greeted him and introduced her companions. "How is Mark feeling?" she asked.

"There is no difference. But I am not here to see him."

She waited to hear. She thought he wasn't going to say any more, and she considered excusing herself so they could talk in private. But apparently he decided that the information would shortly be common knowledge anyhow and that they might just as well get the story accurately. "Dr. Hu has been injured."

"An accident?" Janet asked, knowing even as she heard her own words that the security police did not deal with accidents.

"She was wounded with a knife."

"Like Mary Allen!" gasped Dorothy.

"Dr. Hu is not dead. However, the attacks are similar."

"She was attacked in the clinic? Someone tried to get at Mark!"

"If that is true, what would be the reason for killing both husband and wife?" the officer asked, looking intently at Janet, puzzling about the burst of relief that was palpable in her conclusion.

"It would have to be something about them personally—about them as a family. Something in their life that had nothing to do with China or with any of us here."

"Hm. Perhaps. However, there is no evidence that Mr. Allen was the one targeted. Dr. Hu was attacked some distance from the clinic. Apparently she was on her way home when it happened."

"There really ought to be more lights on the grounds," Dorothy muttered.

"It does not appear that she was attacked from behind—in the dark. She might even have stopped to speak with her assailant. She was stabbed in the chest, facing whoever did it."

"Was she able to tell you who it was?"

"Not yet," he said grimly.

"There goes the theory that Mary was killed by someone who objected to her opinions on population control. Dr. Hu's views couldn't be more different."

"And it's not someone who just doesn't like foreigners." Dorothy blurted that out and then looked embarrassed. She probably thought it seemed rude to mention the endemic Chinese xenophobia when officials were always saying how grateful they were to the foreign experts.

"Will she be all right?" Janet asked.

"The wound was not very serious. One blow and the assailant must have run at the sound of the motorcycle."

"Motorcycle?"

"Yes. Armand Grisson brought her back to the clinic."

Janet's mouth tightened automatically. "What does he say about it?"

"He says nothing."

"I'll bet. Very convenient, his being right there to save her. Did he see someone running away?"

The officer shook his head. "He carried her to a bed and left. No one has seen him."

"Are you sure he didn't attack her?" John asked. "He's very odd."

"Attack her and then save her life? To what purpose?"

He shrugged. "Attack her impulsively and regret it immediately."

Janet swallowed her dislike of the man and tried to be fair. "That would be out of character, I think. His hatreds go deep and fester for a long time. I can't see him doing something violent and then immediately regretting it. He would probably plan his attacks and then, if he were found out, he would boast about them. Have you tried to find him?" she asked the officer.

"I have sent men to search. We will find him."

The clinic director came hurrying toward them and took the officer aside, speaking urgently to him in Chinese. When she was finished and had moved back toward the clinic, the officer told them that there was no change with Dr. Hu, and he said good night before following her. Janet looked after them speculatively. What was the urgency all about? she wondered. If she had been alone she would have gone after them.

Twenty-one

THIS TIME Wang Qu Qing was on the phone, calling from the gate. "I have come to see you."

"Of course, Qu Qing. Come on up."

He hung up and in a few minutes he was sitting in her living room.

"I'm curious, Qu Qing. How did you get in the other day, when I met you outside the building?"

He shrugged. "I say I wish to see the American professor and the soldier permits me to enter."

"But not this time?"

"No. Now he says I must call you before he will permit me to enter. They have not found the murderer of the American writer," he added.

Was this just his usual way of announcing information to prove he had an inside track on what was going on, or was he saying that the soldiers were not always so careful about screening Chinese visitors to the compound?

"Do you think a Chinese killed her—because she was an enemy of China's policy?"

He considered the question carefully, hating to have to say he had no ideas on the subject. "Perhaps a Chinese," he said slowly. "But I think a foreigner."

"You don't believe a Chinese could be a murderer?"

"Chinese have killed Chinese. No one would kill a foreigner."

"Even if the foreigner might do harm to China?"

He smiled. "One person could not do harm. China is very big and powerful."

"She might have done harm to Dr. Chen," Janet insisted.

"Some workers in the laboratory say she wanted Dr. Chen to stop his work. Not to stop. To . . . to . . ."

"To spoil his work? To destroy it?"

"Yes. They say she is a strong woman who talks to him very much."

"Could one of them want to stop her from talking?"

"I do not think so. They also talk much, but they do not kill. It is a terrible crime to kill—and to kill a foreigner . . ." He made a movement with his hand as if to deny categorically that such a crime was conceivable.

If she were to consider the tradition of Chinese law, Janet knew with what aversion the Chinese contemplated violence against other people. To argue, to fight with words, to call one another the most insulting names—these were situations that could be ignored or dealt with by interceding neighbors. But as soon as a blow was landed the police became involved, and the consequences—harassment, fines, the possibility of jail sentences—were scrupulously to be avoided.

Presumably, like any other people, a Chinese could attack in the heat of passion, and even kill. The way Mary was killed. But it would have taken some planning to get through the gate and discover her room number without being identified. That required coolness if the murderer was a stranger to Mary.

But the attack on Dr. Hu seemed to be impulsive. If the aim had been to kill her, it had been aborted because of the time and place of the attack—and so probably had not been carefully planned. Were two people involved in knifing the population? She thought not. This kind of coincidence could not be accepted as a working hypothesis.

"Did you know that Dr. Hu has been attacked with a knife?" she asked Qu Qing.

"Yes. The soldiers at the gate were speaking of it. I heard them. She is not killed."

"No, that's right. But she's very seriously injured. Why would someone want to hurt her?"

He looked at her without answering. Why indeed? It made no sense at all. If Mary was murdered by someone who wanted to keep her from doing harm to the research, why would that same person try to murder someone who could not be more totally committed to the work? It made no sense at all—unless the reason for killing had nothing to do with the research.

But what else did Dr. Hu and Mary have in common? They had hardly ever spoken to each other.

Qu Qing broke in on her thoughts. "I must go now, Professor. I will see you again."

"Oh yes, Qu Qing. I'm glad you came. Do come again."

"Perhaps the security police will find the murderer soon—if you will help them."

She smiled absently. She knew he hadn't much faith in the ability of the police, and far too much faith in hers.

She went out with him. A little air before bed might help clear her head. It was a lovely night—a black sky dotted with diamonds, the air still mild. Qu Qing got his bicycle from the parking shed and walked, wheeling it as they went, toward the gate.

"You will come to the college tomorrow?"

"Why, no, I wasn't planning to. Why do you ask?"

"I would like for you to see my teaching." For once he seemed diffident, almost shy. "I am trying to teach your ways. You will come to watch?"

She smiled, feeling again the fondness that had become a part of their relationship when she first met him. "Yes, I'll come and watch you teach. I'm honored that you use my methods."

He mounted his bicycle, waved and rode off, and she turned back to the hotel.

Ian Chen passed her in his car and stopped in front of her hotel, waiting for her to catch up. "Hi," he said. "Are you all right?"

"I suppose so," she answered, twisting her mouth into a wry smile. "I guess you've heard about Dr. Hu."

"Yes. They called me right after it happened. I think she'll come out of it. She's very strong."

"Have you any idea why someone would want to kill her?"

Slowly he got out of the car and stood leaning against it. "Why," he asked, "would anyone want to kill either one of them?"

"You know, that Armand Grisson is pretty weird. Could he have some insane idea about blaming a series of murders on a mysterious lunatic?"

"You mean just kill people at random?" he asked doubtfully.

"Not exactly. I mean, maybe he wanted to get rid of Mary with some crazy idea of saving China from interfering foreigners. Then attacking Dr. Hu to confuse the investigators. He may be crazy but I don't think he's stupid. He may be quite capable of such devious planning."

"What about Carol?" he asked.

She felt the blood drain from her face. "Wh-what d-do you m-mean?"

"Hasn't she talked to you about it?"

"About what?"

"Carol's afraid of the Algerian. He's threatened her."

Janet moved to lean against the car beside him. She knew her knees felt weak, but she couldn't have said why. "Threatened her with what?"

"I'm not quite sure. Something about getting out of China before starting to write about the country's policies. He seemed to imply that the same thing could happen to her as happened to Mary."

Janet gasped. "Have you told this to the police?"

"Carol said she would report it. And that she wouldn't be going out alone at night—or letting anyone into her room. I was just going up to see how she's feeling."

They walked up the steps together and went into the lobby. The desk clerk sat faithfully at her post; there would be no strangers coming and going at will for a long time. She actually greeted them by name; apparently she had seen Ian go up on other occasions.

He stopped at Carol's door and knocked. When Carol opened, Janet waved and smiled and went on to her own room. Obviously no one had attacked her yet; she even seemed cheerful as she smiled and called out a hearty "Hi" to Janet's back before she let Ian in.

It was not until several hours later, when Janet was just falling asleep over a book, that a frightened Carol tapped softly at her door and asked to come in.

Twenty-two

"PLEASE, JANET. Come with me."

"Carol, it's not a good idea, meeting him in an empty building."

"But what if he's telling the truth about knowing who killed Mary?"

"Why doesn't he go to the police?"

"He just won't. Something about the police being incompetent, or that they won't believe him. I don't know. And he particularly said for you to come too. He thinks you've got a pipeline to the police and that you're in a good position to use the information he has."

"When did you see him—speak to him?"

"He phoned me a few minutes ago. After Ian left and I was alone. He must have been watching for Ian to leave."

"Watching from where?" There were no public phones on the grounds, and Grisson's apartment—from which he would probably have to phone—was some distance away. Surely not within sight of the hotel entrance.

Carol brushed the question away impatiently. "If you won't come with me, I'll meet him alone. I—I'm n-not afraid." She looked terrified.

"Okay. I'll leave a message at the desk for the officer. Just in case."

"Hurry! He said come immediately. I don't want him to change his mind." Her fear seemed to be gone, and she was very excited

—beautiful in her excitement. The red hair seemed to bounce with its own life and her skin glowed. The lovely turquoise scarf around her neck picked up the color of her eyes and complemented the tones of her hair and skin. So beautiful that even through the pall of worry and doubt that dragged her down Janet couldn't help appreciating the picture she made.

She stopped at the desk and got the worker to understand that she wanted paper and pen, while Carol fumed and grimaced impatiently. Even as she wrote, Janet wondered what the point was: if they were going to be murdered for their stupidity, no one would get the note until morning—if then. The officer might not come into the building, and it was not likely that anyone would seek him out to deliver a note addressed to the "Security Police Officer." Why in hell did she never think to ask his name when she saw him? And why did he never offer it? What a curious relationship they had. She couldn't remember ever knowing anyone at home the way she knew him and not having a name to go with the person.

The store that sold cheese and cookies, and sometimes bread and liverwurst, was in the basement of a building that housed a dining room that served Western food. Set down between one of the hotels and the recreation building, it seemed somehow more isolated than it actually was. Perhaps it was because it so often was unused—the dining room closed for lack of customers, and the other stores closed out of regular hours.

Oddly, the door to the building was never locked. Once, looking to buy a bar of soap, she had gone into the basement at the wrong time and walked the long, dimly lit corridor of closed stores to the small one that sold thread and soap and other notions and toiletries. Her heels echoed on the concrete floor, and the rough stone walls and dank air made her think of stories of medieval dungeons. An atavistic fear of being locked in sent a shudder through her and she had suddenly found herself running toward the door. Once she was outside she had forgotten what had made her run, what she had been afraid of.

Now, even though Carol was at her side, the cold, dark corridor was not inviting.

"Why in the world would he want to meet us here?" she asked Carol irritably.

"You know he's cuckoo. There's no understanding why he thinks the way he does. But he certainly was serious about knowing something important about Mary's murder."

"There isn't a soul around down here. The stores are all closed. I'm getting out."

"Oh, please, Janet. Don't. If we leave now we may never know what he's got to say. He won't speak to the police."

"If he wants to speak to me, he can damned well do it out in the open. I see no reason why I should cater to his craziness."

As they spoke, they kept walking, Carol taking the lead and setting a brisk pace. They came to an unexplainable cul-de-sac at right angles to the corridor. There was nothing in it, just a sort of hollowing-out of the corridor wall, not large enough for a store, darker than the rest of the area. Armand stood there, leaning against the far wall, wearing his long white coat. In the dimness the dirt on the coat was obscured. Only the white showed, and several inches below it the unbelievable white boots he affected.

"*Alors*, let us talk," he said as soon as they saw him. "Have you decided to leave China to solve her own problems?" he demanded of Carol.

"That's none of your business," Carol retorted.

"Then there is nothing to say!" he shouted into her face. "You are as evil as the other one! You Americans think you can tell the world how to live. Well, we will not permit it. You will be stopped. I have a way to stop you."

In the dark the two of them seemed to Janet to be locked in physical combat, the Algerian's arms upraised menacingly and Carol's reaching for—or fastened on—his face. Janet grabbed at Carol and tried to pull her away. She put her own hands around Carol's arm, at the elbow, and hung on. The arm unbent and one hand moved in a backswing made steely by tennis and regular swimming. The hand connected with Janet's nose and she was out cold.

When she opened her eyes, she was lying on the cold concrete with her head resting against the rough wall, her hands tied behind her. Carol and Armand weren't there. The corridor was silent.

The cold of the floor came through her clothes and numbed her side. With her hands tied behind her, she couldn't lie on her back; it made her shoulders crack and feel as if her arms were being pulled out of their sockets.

She saw movement near the wall and she froze from much more than the cold. She shuddered long and agonizingly and thought she could feel each individual hair on the skin of her body tighten, responding to the ancient biological signal for flight. Only she couldn't run.

Her eyes strained in the half-light, so wide that the muscles behind them ached. She felt herself beginning to scream but tried to suppress it. The sound of her own scream would be the final straw, and she would lose herself in wild, insane panic. In panic, tied down and unable to run, she was sure that her mind would go. Only in severing herself completely from this horror could she survive.

Suddenly she laughed at herself, and the sound echoed around the stone walls of the corridor. She certainly was powerless to "sever" her body from the predicament. The only alternative was to sever her mind. Okay, she agreed. Do I scream and go crazy with panic or do I deliberately turn off my mind and go quietly and rationally crazy? She laughed again. Maybe she would survive this after all—body and mind. Maybe there was a way out. At least she knew she hadn't gone to pieces yet.

The thought of what moved in the corners she pushed away. She even shook her head, like a fighter trying to clear the effects of a hard punch. She needed clarity if she was going to get out of this. Without thinking she started to put one hand up to her head, and the tug on the rope loosened it at once. Armand had tied her very carelessly! She felt an instant of pure joy, but then she was afraid again. This time the fear that gripped her was no throwback to a primitive fear of darkness and solitude. Something had happened to Carol. The crazy Algerian had dragged her off—maybe to kill her the way he had killed Mary—in a fit of frustration and fury.

She struggled to her feet and leaned her head against the rough wall, grateful for the cold dampness that helped dissipate the blackness that threatened to close over her again. Her face felt funny, deformed. She touched gingerly at the soreness for a moment and then started to move. She wanted to run, but her feet felt magnetized to the floor and she could move only heavily and with enormous awkwardness toward the exit. She knew that she must get help.

Outside, she turned to the right toward the hotel, hoping the police were there. Her eyes adjusted to the early morning light and she saw the officer coming out of the clinic building beyond her hotel. She ran toward him and then could only cling to him, unable to catch her breath.

He led her back into the clinic and sat her down. But she was up again immediately. "No, no! There isn't time! It's that lunatic, Grisson. He's got Carol. He's going to kill her! The way he killed Mary!"

"Where?" he asked tensely.

"Where the stores are. In the basement." She pointed vaguely, exhausted. "Hurry! Hurry!" And she tried to drag him out.

He took hold of her shoulders and spoke into her face. "He is not the murderer. He killed no one."

"There's no time!" she yelled, still trying to move toward the door.

"Listen to me. The Algerian is innocent. He killed no one. Do you hear me? He is not a murderer."

Slowly her eyes began to focus on him and she understood what he was saying. A little more calmly, she insisted, "But he's got Carol. He's taken her someplace. He was furious with her. He looked capable of murder."

"Stay here, I will find them." And he sat her down again and started out.

But she wouldn't have it. She'd really lose her mind sitting there wondering what had happened. "No. I'm going with you."

He paid her no attention, just strode out, motioning a soldier outside to follow him. Janet went after them both, though the distance between her and the soldiers widened quickly.

When she got to the stores building, the door had already closed behind them. She went into the dim passage, rushing to catch up to the sound of their heavy shoes on the concrete. It was amazing how harmless the place seemed now. Even in the poor light she could see quite clearly. It was just a basement shopping mall. Even though the shops were all closed and no other people were around, there was obviously nothing in the least menacing about the place.

The two men were coming back toward her, having found no one—not Carol, not Armand Grisson.

"Where can he have taken her?" Her anxiety about Carol's safety made her sound harshly demanding. Also, the pain in her face did nothing to contribute to either optimism or patience.

"There is no reason to fear for Miss Walker's safety," the officer assured her. "The man is not dangerous."

"What are you saying? He lured us down here and he's done something to Carol!"

"Calm yourself. We will search for them. But he is not the murderer of Mrs. Allen. It was her husband who arranged for her murder."

"Mark?" She stopped short and stared at him. "How do you know?"

"He has confessed this to me. The sight of the murder scene was more than he expected to see. It has broken all his resolve."

"I don't understand."

"He hired an assassin to kill her."

Janet put her hand to her eyes to still the whirl of feelings. "You must find Carol. Why would she leave me lying unconscious if he didn't make her leave against her will?"

"Come," he said. "We will take you to your rooms. Then we will find her."

"No. I want to go with you."

"Very well. But you appear to be exhausted. And your face needs treatment."

"Later," she said firmly. "I want to be sure Carol is safe."

Fleetingly she wondered what reason Mark had given for having his wife murdered. In a curious way she could almost respect

—at least empathize with—murder in the heat of passion. But cold-bloodedly contracting for a killing was vile, evil. That human reason should be used to justify such a corrupt act outraged her.

In the end, they had no trouble finding Carol—and Armand. The officer led the way to Armand's apartment, in the same building where Ian lived. They were both there, Carol huddled in a corner of the bedroom crying hysterically, and Armand dead on the bed, a knife in his chest.

Twenty-three

BETWEEN THEM, Janet and the officer had gotten Carol off the floor and into a chair in the living room. She was still incoherent, but her crying was getting softer and some of what she was saying began to be understandable.

"He wanted to kill me," she sobbed. "Crazy! He was crazy! He said I would destroy China. Like Mary."

Finally they were able to get from her an account of what had happened. Janet lay on the cold cement of the shops area. Armand grabbed Carol's arm and forced her to tie Janet's hands with a piece of string he took from the pocket of his coat and then to walk out of the building and across the compound to his apartment. The knife he held to her side kept her quiet, in fear of her life.

Once at home, he locked the door behind them and began to "talk crazy." He said he would kill her and everyone else who tried to wrest countries from their rightful citizens. He had stopped Mary Allen, and now he would stop her from continuing Mary's work.

She tried to reason with him, telling him that she was not committed to Mary Allen's point of view, that she believed in a better world for everyone. She told him that China was doing the right thing, that it just needed to do more in concert with the other countries of the world.

But he was past listening. His eyes stared wildly and he even foamed at the mouth. He never let go of her arm, and now he held her while he raised the knife above his head. In another second he would plunge it into her.

Struggling frantically, trying to keep his arm from descending, she lost all sense of time and place; she was totally consumed with the effort to keep that knife from moving toward her. Somehow he tripped backward and fell, and she fell with him. Her hands, clamped with desperate strength on his arm, came down, and the knife in his hand tore into his chest.

The force of the blow must have been incredibly strong. No part of the blade showed; it had penetrated right up to the hilt.

The officer and Janet listened to the account. He asked no questions, just looked somberly at the tearful woman. For a while Janet felt sick and exhausted, grateful only that she and Carol were alive.

Carol had finished and put her head back and closed her eyes, while the officer began to set in motion the machinery for officially noting another death and starting the investigation. He had taken in the story and not even nodded at the end of it. Only turned away to give an order to the soldier with him.

What was going on in his mind? Was he satisfied that the whole business was finished? Was Mark . . . ? Mark!

She remembered what the officer had been telling her while she tried desperately to get him to find Carol. Mark had confessed! She closed her eyes. She was in no condition for this, and she didn't want to think about it. Getting up, she looked toward the officer, hoping he would let her return to her own rooms. She wanted to lock the door and get into bed and pull the covers over her head. She didn't want to think about murder anymore. Especially not about murder to which two people had confessed.

Oddly, as she asked for permission to leave, she did not ask to be allowed to take Carol back to the hotel with her. Ordinarily she would have felt more protective of her friend than that.

The officer did let her go and, once out of the door, she ran into Ian Chen. Literally. He held her to prevent her falling over with the impact, but as soon as she regained her balance she threw off his arms. Not until he spoke was she aware with whom she had collided.

"What's wrong, Janet? Why are the police here? Is Carol all right?"

She peered into his face as if she was having difficulty focusing, as if everything she saw was blurred. "I don't know," she said clearly.

"What's happened?" He looked over her shoulder to the building and the police car, but he didn't move. Why wasn't he running to see for himself what had happened? "Has there been another murder?"

"I don't know," she said again.

He grabbed her by the shoulders as if he was going to shake her. "What the hell do you mean, you don't know? What's going on up there?"

She shook him off again and muttered, "Go see for yourself." Stepping quickly around him, she went on to the hotel and up the steps without looking back.

After all that, she didn't get into bed. Somehow she felt that would make her more vulnerable. She wanted to be dressed, on her feet. She stood looking out of the window and saw Ian, Carol and the officer coming along the path. Ian had his arm around Carol, even though she seemed quite capable of walking on her own. All three disappeared into the hotel, and in a few minutes someone knocked at her door.

"It is not too late to speak?" the officer asked.

"No, it's not too late. Please come in."

They sat in the plastic easy chairs and she poured him a glass of the excellent sherry she had bought in one of the stores on the compound. "I'm glad you came up," she told him. "I didn't want to sleep."

"You are very unhappy about the death of the Algerian?"

She sighed deeply. "The Algerian, Dr. Hu, Mary. It's all too much."

"You do not think that this is the end of it? You expect more murder—still another attack?"

She shook her head. "It doesn't feel finished," she muttered. Then, looking at him sharply, "Do *you* think it's over?"

He sipped from his glass and did not answer her question directly. "A recorded confession from the Algerian would have been most desirable."

"Yes, I would have wanted to hear from him why he felt it was necessary to attack Dr. Hu."

He nodded.

They sat silently for a while. She pictured Mary—tall, broadshouldered, she had carried herself proudly, purposefully, in spite of all the opposition she faced. And she was charming. Good men had loved her.

In a way she was not unlike Carol. Both were large women, long-legged, attractive. But with quite different coloring—one flashing; the other cool. Mary had mentioned something at dinner that evening about exercising regularly, about how important it was for someone who did so much sitting in cars and planes and ate so much hotel food. And Carol had said she kept fit by swimming and playing tennis. Both of them strong, healthy women.

"Armand Grisson was such a small, slight man. How did he ever manage to overpower Carol and force her to come with him? How could he have gotten close enough to her even with a knife?" She touched her nose. "One swipe from that muscular arm and he would have been knocked as senseless as I was." It would have been no great feat for Carol to turn Armand's knife on himself, she thought. "She said he tripped backward and she fell with him?"

"That is what she said."

"It *could* have happened that way." With whom was she arguing? It was over, wasn't it? "How do you think he got out of Mary's room without being seen?"

"It was early in the morning. It was possible that, for a moment or two, there was no one to see him."

"Maybe he used his coat to hide the bloodstains." She pursed her lips, doubt written large on her face. "Stupid. He took the coat off before he killed her?"

"Perhaps. If he knew her well."

"Then you think he was the one who was seen coming out by the desk clerk?"

He shrugged. "The clerk was certain he was not the one."

"And the screaming? Why did no one hear her scream?"

"It is possible that she did not scream. Shock at the first cut could have silenced her while she fought desperately for her life. That can happen to some people. There are those who scream immediately when threatened—and often save their lives. Others become silent, unable to make a sound."

But there was no satisfaction for either of them in the solution. Two people were dead, one lay near death and after all the killer had betrayed himself. No clear thinking or dogged police work had brought him down. Not satisfying at all. At least that was what she thought was depressing them both.

But that still left Mark's confession. What had all that been about? Surely he and Armand Grisson had no connection with each other. She wasn't even sure that they had ever met.

"No, it was another matter—the desire to have his wife dead. She refused to permit the divorce. A strong-minded woman."

"She wanted the marriage? What did they have together?"

"It was convenient for her. She thought the people she spoke for wanted her to be married."

She made a sound—a hoot? Did anyone still believe that marriage made a woman respectable? "She refused to give Mark a divorce because, for the moment, it was what she wanted. She kept people available for her purposes. Only Ian Chen doesn't know that."

By the time Mark was out of the hospital and on his feet again, the matter of the assassin was cleared up. For a banker and businessman, Mark was surprisingly naive about handing out money. For once his eagerness to close a deal had betrayed his usual prudence and he had paid a generous sum to a drifter he had encountered in one of the free markets dotted around Beijing. He was easily identifiable—an unshaven, dirty man who seemed to have no business at the market. He wandered from stall to stall, joining in the conversation wherever two or more people talked. Mark had watched him for hours, followed him about, until it was clear he had no home and no apparent means of support.

Such people were almost nonexistent in China, a country where everyone must belong to a work group—or at least a family—to survive, a bureaucracy where every function was duly recorded, even if not always officially approved. Occasionally a man would leave the countryside to come to the city without permission and became one of the "unofficial workers" who picked up odd jobs for very little pay. But people did not sleep in the streets of Beijing or stand on street corners begging for a handout, the way they did now on the streets of New York and Philadelphia.

Mark, with his fluency in Chinese, convinced the man to take his money and, with the promise of more after the deed was done, described Mary to him and told him where she lived and something of her schedule. He had no wish to know where or how she would be eliminated; he only wanted her stopped, out of his life, out of Ian's life.

If he had not been so shocked at the murder scene, he would have realized that the assassin could not have found his way into Mary's room unobserved. Earlier, with more astuteness, he might have known that, just because someone was a rare misfit in society, it didn't mean he was also willing to kill another person.

So the "assassin" took the money and ran. The police found him. This is relatively easy in a tightly organized society. He had been several hundred miles into the countryside the night Mary was murdered. A whole village was able to substantiate his alibi.

Twenty-four

CHINA IS A COUNTRY officially proud of its minorities. Although regional and historical prejudices exist and there are low rumblings at the subtle efforts to minimize the use of minority languages and customs, the official policy is to provide all groups with opportunities for education and political representation. Entertainments often feature minority groups in their traditional costumes performing dances and songs of surprising cultural variety. Some are more Slavic than Chinese. Others remind one of the dances and rhythms of India. Such dance troupes have toured not only in their own country but in many other countries, to a delighted reception by audiences that have been led to expect only drabness and humorless ideology from the Chinese.

What all the minority cultures have in common, however, are the bright and varied colors of their costumes. It is a wonder that, in recent years, the Chinese people have been able to suppress their love for bright colors as completely as they do, dressing themselves in dull blues and grays. But very small children continue to be dressed brightly, suggesting to the psychologist that the penchant for colors will survive in every generation and one day soon will burst forth again in all the glory of the imperial court.

In the midst of the unsolved mysteries of murder and mayhem, the invitation came to attend a presentation of minority songs and dances in the Cultural Palace of Nationalities on West Chang'an

Avenue. On Tuesday, Janet, dissatisfied as she was, felt obliged to respond. Official functions were always well attended, no matter how reluctant people were to engage in frivolity at a particular moment.

After a morning in classes—Carol in her own and Janet in Qu Qing's—they went back to the Friendship Hotel for lunch. Afternoon classes were canceled and a car was sent from the college for them. Dorothy and John Peter piled in too. It was no surprise to them to meet Ian Chen walking up the steps of the Cultural Palace when they arrived.

Dozens of buses were disgorging laughing, expectant people for the event, many foreigners but mostly Chinese. Even the officer was there, standing near a wall in the enormous lobby, smoking a cigarette and looking much too sober in the midst of all the laughing and noise.

Ian said something to him in Chinese and they laughed. "It is our duty," the officer answered in English, "to encourage our people, to make them proud of their history. You will enjoy the dances."

"It's the costumes I love," said Janet. "The red satins and gold. It makes the whole thing very exciting."

"You have seen this before?"

"I've seen several entertainments by minorities. They show a side of China we never see in everyday Beijing. I love the spectacle of it."

The officer looked pleased and puzzled at the same time, struggling between the pleasure he got from a foreigner's approval of things Chinese and surprise that such unsophisticated and old-fashioned entertainments could impress the American professor.

He told the group to wait until the crush toward the entrance had diminished, and he would take them to seats at the front of the room where they would have an unobstructed view of the stage.

"Reserved seats?" Dorothy laughed. Such a bourgeois idea in Communist China.

"Some seats left empty for busy officials who may enter late,"

the officer explained, refusing to acknowledge the obvious favor-
itism for the privileged.

Dorothy nodded but her eyes danced. She recognized better
than most how prone human beings were to fooling themselves.
But they all appreciated the good seats and being able to avoid the
sharp elbows on their way in. Janet settled back to enjoy the
performance, grateful that for one of the few times in her life she
didn't have to crane her neck around someone in the seat in front
of her. It was only those times when she went to the theater that
she was reminded that she was only five feet tall.

She sat next to Carol, with the officer on her right. If there were
any spoken parts, he could translate for her. Ian, on the other side
of Carol, could provide any necessary explanation for her, and the
officer, on whose right Dorothy sat could also explain things to
her and John.

The show was everything Janet could have wished—happy,
lively dances by red-cheeked boys and girls, some pantomime that
communicated easily in a universal tongue, and the minor-key
music that so bothered some Western ears but which made Janet
smile, especially as she watched the musicians casually sawing
away on the strings without sheet music or a conductor to follow.

Janet leaned toward Carol. "Aren't the costumes attractive?"
she exclaimed. "Just look at those colors!"

"Colors just made for *you,* Janet. Not for me."

"Well, I wasn't thinking of clothes for myself, any more than I
think of clothes when I look at a painting."

"I think people respond to colors anywhere in the same way. If
they like them, if the colors make them feel good, they appreciate
the objects that have those colors. In painting, costumes, the
clothes they wear."

"You know, that's an interesting idea. I've had red dresses and,
once, a gold dress. And I loved them!"

Carol smiled. "My colors are lavenders and greens. I'd never
wear any of these colors. Even seeing them on the stage leaves me
cold."

Janet looked back to the stage, its exciting movements and

rushes of color and swirling bodies and kicking feet. How could all that movement and energy and sparkle leave an observer cold?

"I'll bet," she said to Carol, "you'd create a sensation in some shades of red."

"Ugh. Never! My colors range from cool to cold. I look awful in anything else."

"Would you like to hear the story of this dance?" asked the officer from her other side.

She nodded and smiled as she listened to the usual tale of unrequited love that triumphed in the end. The stories were all so naive and romantic. The dances and costumes were, too, but somehow that seemed all right to her. Maybe it was because her own knowledge of costume and dance was rather elementary, whereas human behavior was, for her, a profound and complex study.

At the intermission they rose to stretch their legs. Dorothy and John offered to bring them all refreshments from the carts in the street. They returned with bottles of orange liquid. Janet made a face when she saw the bright orange color that stained lips, tongue and teeth, and started to say that here was a warm color that almost matched Carol's hair.

In the middle of her observation, the words died away. She was standing a little apart with the officer—the others talking among themselves. He raised his eyebrows and waited. "It's all wrong," she said wonderingly.

He said nothing.

"The colors were all wrong."

And suddenly she knew what had really happened. It was not that no one had been seen going to Mary's room, implying that the murderer had managed to come and go unnoticed. The truth was that Carol had been the only one there. No one else could have gotten away in blood-splattered clothes. But Carol had merely changed into Mary's clothes, rolled her own up into an inconspicuous bundle, and walked out the way she had come. Mary's clothes fit her perfectly—except for one thing. The colors were all wrong. Mary's gray hair was beautifully complemented by her pearly gray blouses and red print scarves. No redhead with Carol's coloring would ever be caught dead in that shade of gray.

The officer saw in her expression that something momentous had occurred to her and he put his hand on her arm, cautioning her to wait until a more appropriate time. She nodded her understanding. This was not the place to accuse someone of murder—certainly not someone as volatile as Carol. It might result in a spectacular scene, with thousands of curious people milling about to hear what was going on.

So she sat for the second act, quiet on the surface but agonizing inside. Maybe she was wrong. Maybe Carol had a good explanation for wearing a gray blouse and skirt and a red scarf the morning she had come to her room to talk about Ian. She had been on her way to meet with Mary, she said, to plan the series of articles in collaboration. She had looked so tired, so colorless. Almost ugly —as ugly as anyone with her regular features and gorgeous hair could look. Janet remembered thinking that, but it was not until after Carol had discovered the murder, and Janet had attributed her appearance to the shock of finding the body. But she had looked the same earlier, only it hadn't registered. Janet remembered only that she had been concerned about her friend.

Now she really had something to be concerned about.

Twenty-five

ON THE WAY OUT Janet and the officer walked behind the rest, Janet murmuring quickly that they should all meet back at the Friendship Hotel. When Carol got into Ian's car the officer bent at the window to say something to Ian, then got into his jeep while Janet, Dorothy and John looked for their car. They saw the driver wander out of the entrance to the Cultural Palace; he had gone in to see the dances too.

All the way back Janet could hear Dorothy talking enthusiastically but she didn't make out a word of what she was saying. When they all got out at Dorothy's building, Dorothy was laughing. "I *do* like to have the stage to myself," she said, "but you've never been so willing to let me do all the talking." Then, getting a good look at Janet's face, "Are you all right?"

"Yes. No. Come along, will you?"

Mystified, they followed her; for once Dorothy didn't ask questions.

They all sat in the easy chairs in the lobby. Even those who had no idea what this was all about were silent, uneasy. Carol seemed no different from the rest, though she peered thoughtfully first at one face, then another. Ian wasn't there and Janet wondered where he had gone—if he had expected something terrible and begged off.

"I'm sorry, Carol," Janet said finally.

"Sorry?" She said it brightly, as if nothing could be so serious, and she was ready to forgive any slight transgression.

"You saw Mary before you came to my room that morning," she said, her voice firm but very low.

"When?" Again, the question seemed ingenuous, as if she had no idea what Janet was talking about.

"Mary was murdered early Saturday morning. After that you came to my room. Then you went to her room again and 'found' her."

"No!" she protested loudly. "You can't believe that! Mary was my friend."

"Ian is your friend. Mary was a threat to him."

"No! She wasn't. She was his friend too."

"More than just a friend, maybe?" Janet made the question purposely provocative.

"That's a filthy thing to say! Ian loves me!"

"He knew Mary long before he met you."

"Mary had Mark!"

"Maybe Mary wanted more—Mark and Ian and—"

"No! That's not true!" Suddenly she calmed down and took a different tack. "You're being ridiculous," she sneered. "Everyone knows the front doors of the hotels are locked at night. Don't tell me you believe I picked the lock to get into Mary's room!"

Janet had no answer to that, except to turn mutely to the desk clerk. There must be an explanation. She was certain that, somehow, Carol had gotten into the hotel and into Mary's room. But the clerk just stared back at her, at a loss. With the little English he had, he was obviously not able to follow the talk. Nevertheless he took a stab at participating; he wouldn't have been Chinese if he had kept out of the conversation altogether. "Cadre have key," he said. Apparently he had understood a word or two—or at least the word "lock."

"Yes," Janet said slowly. "The cadre locks the door at night."

"Yes, yes. Cadre locks door. Opens in morning." He was delighted to have understood the sentence.

Janet smiled absently at his enthusiasm. Without thinking, her teacher instinct wanted to encourage him in his use of English.

"At what time does he lock the door at night?" she asked, again enunciating each word very clearly.

"I know! Locks at twelve hours. Yes, twelve hours."

She hardly heard his answer, but she asked another question he could understand. "At what time does he open the door in the morning?"

"Yes! He opens in morning 4 A.M."

She smiled and nodded and started to commend his English. Then, "What time?"

"Time?"

"In the morning, when does the cadre unlock the door?"

It was too fast for him. He became confused and started to stutter. The officer interceded and asked the question in Chinese and the man answered, *"Sidian-zhong."* Four o'clock. He asked another question and the clerk gave a longer answer.

"He says the cadre unlocks both hotels before he is awake. The cadre has much to do in the mornings. He unlocks the doors and then goes to do other things."

The officer and Janet looked at each other and then turned to Carol.

"No!" she shouted again. "I came right from Ian to my room. I told you. I went to my room."

"Yes. You also told me that it was still dark out when you came out of Ian's flat." Janet felt awful. "It starts getting light at about five. You left Ian before five in the morning."

Carol's jaw sagged in dismay. In her need to confide in Janet she had forgotten her description of the compound deserted in the early morning just before light. But she quickly rallied. "No," she said again. "Ask Ian. He'll tell you I was with him all night. Until I came to see you—to talk to you."

"You were wearing a gray blouse and a red scarf, Carol—"

"I thought you were my friend! Why don't you help me?" she wailed.

Janet bit her lip. "Oh, Carol, I *am* your friend. I want to help you." She really meant it. What she did not mean was that she would help Carol cover up what she had done. Her friend needed help. She also needed to be stopped. "Carol, did you come right to my room from Ian's apartment or did you stop at your room first? Which did you do?"

"This time I'm telling the truth. I came right to your room."

"You were with Ian until then, from the time you dropped me off?"

"Yes, yes," she said eagerly. "You believe me now, don't you?"

"All right, Carol. Don't worry about it. You go with the officer and we'll straighten it out." She turned beseechingly to him.

With characteristic sensitivity he understood and said something to his aide, then to Carol: "Go with him to the clinic and rest there. I will come soon to speak with you again."

When they had left Janet thanked him for his consideration. "I feel so sorry . . ."

"Yes," he agreed. "You are certain now?"

"Oh yes. Certain. You can check with Ian Chen if you like. But that night she was wearing a turquoise blouse that matched her eyes—a most unusual color. And a white skirt. If she went right to his apartment as she says and then came to my rooms, she had no opportunity to change her clothes."

"She must be very confused if she could not provide a better story for herself. She might have left Dr. Chen earlier and taken the time to change her clothes before she came to your room."

"She must have decided to say that at first, until she saw that I realized she was wearing the wrong colors. I suppose she hopes Ian will support her story."

"Do you believe he will?"

"No. He's already troubled about her behavior. He knows there's something very wrong."

Ian came in then. He saw the serious faces but everyone was seated, apparently having a quiet discussion. "Dr. Hu is coming along," he announced. "I'm sure she'll be all right. She's a brave woman."

"Was she able to speak to you?" asked the officer.

"Oh no. She's still very weak. She wanted to talk but I wouldn't let her. Anyway, I thought she'd better talk to you first. She can probably describe the attack."

"And the attacker?"

"And the attacker. I told her the whole thing was over and the compound was safe again. Her eyes closed in relief." He looked around. "Where's Carol?"

"Where she is safe. There are questions she must answer."

"You have no right to detain her!"

"You must have missed her," Janet tried to soothe him. "She's at the clinic."

He started to leave. "I came out the side entrance; it's closer. What's she doing there?"

No one answered. He turned back. "Hey, what's wrong?"

"Ian, be reasonable," Janet begged. "You know you've been worried about her."

He nodded, and he hid his misery. "What do you want to ask me?"

The officer deferred to Janet. Since she had been one of the party the night before the murder, she could ask the necessary questions with the authority of an eyewitness.

"Ian, when we said good night, did you and Carol go immediately to your place?"

He glanced at the officer and frowned. Then he asked Janet, "Why are you asking me? She was right here; she could have answered that question."

"Please, Ian. This has nothing to do with the way you and Carol feel about each other."

"What does she say?" he insisted.

"She told me she was with you. We just want to verify the times that were involved."

"Yes," he said reluctantly. "We went to my place."

"And when did she leave?"

He hesitated. The Chinese attitude could be contagious after a while. Unmarried men and women just didn't spend the night together. Finally his good sense reasserted itself. He could see the impending doom—he had sensed its presence some time ago.

"She left at about four in the morning."

"Can you remember how she was dressed?"

"Dressed? What the hell does that matter?"

"It matters, Ian. Can you tell us what she was wearing?"

He shrugged. "A dress—no, a blouse." His mouth softened. "It matched her eyes."

Janet put her hand on his arm, then turned to the officer. The question he asked surprised her. It had not been so long ago that psychiatry was thought of as bourgeois and revisionist. "You are a physician, Chen. You had no reason ever to be concerned about Miss Walker's behavior?"

Ian looked startled too. "Concerned? H-how do you mean?"

"She did not seem to you to be . . . uh . . . confused? Disturbed?"

For a long time he didn't answer, as if he was culling his memory for the questions he had asked himself since he had met Carol. Then, "I'm not a psychiatrist." His manner was brusque. He wanted an end to this.

But the officer was not to be put off. He waited for him to say more.

"What are you trying to tell me? Are you saying that Carol murdered Mary? That she attacked Dr. Hu?"

"Yes." Janet's voice was firm. Surely as a scientist he would know that the sharp scalpel was preferable to the dull knife of platitudes and kind lies.

He didn't argue with her. He must have known that this moment was inevitable.

"Ian, tell me again what teachers at San Francisco State said about her."

For a long time he just stared at her. She could see his face grow white as the blood left it.

"Tell me."

"What did they say about her mental state?" He shook his head as if to clear it. "Th-they s-said . . . they said she was brilliant." The last word came out defiantly.

"Yes. And what else?"

He sighed. "I think I knew then," he said quietly. "Th-they said she was . . . was . . . erratic. Brilliant. But erratic. Events . . . they could never . . . never predict . . . which way she would jump. I wanted to think that her knowledge, her incisive thinking frightened them—that they just couldn't handle a woman who wasn't afraid of them. I tried not to remember the times when I couldn't follow her—when she frightened *me*. And they said she was confused. And tired. A-and maybe, maybe very sick.

"I'm going to her. I want to see her."

Suddenly they heard screaming and shouting from outside. They all froze for a heartbeat of time and then dashed to the door. The officer was the first one down the steps and running.

Outside the front door of the clinic Carol, a policeman and the hospital director were struggling together. Wordless shouts came from the man as he tried to hold on to Carol, who was screaming wildly. From the director came a steady stream of words in a high-pitched voice as she also hung on to Carol's wildly flailing arm.

The officer reached them and immediately managed to get behind Carol and lock his arms around her, fastening her arms to her sides and effectively preventing her from moving. The policeman stepped back and put a hand to his red, sweaty face and then took it away to stare at the blood from the scratches on his cheek. The director kept talking until the officer said something, and she ran into the clinic.

In a couple of minutes she was back with a hypodermic syringe and, ignoring Carol's screams, plunged the needle into her arm. Slowly the screams died away as Ian stood by and watched helplessly. When her knees seemed to give way, he lifted her away from the officer and carried her into the clinic. Janet, Dorothy and John still stood frozen and horrified halfway between the hotel and the clinic and watched the officer walk slowly back toward them.

"What happened?" Janet asked.

"The director told her that Dr. Hu would recover."

Twenty-six

BY THE TIME the tranquilizer had taken effect and Carol had stopped screaming, Janet and the officer were entering the clinic. Dorothy and John had wandered off holding hands, as if they needed some comfort from each other—away from tragedy and hysteria.

As Janet and the officer approached the director's office, they heard Mark asking, "Why Mary? What did she ever do to you?"

Mark had apparently felt well enough to get out of bed. He was standing in the doorway that led to the dispensary, and he was looking at Carol. She sat, beautiful, calm, in an easy chair. Ian sat in another, his chair turned toward her. He was looking over his shoulder at Mark, who must have overheard their conversation. A policeman stood behind Carol's chair frowning, seeming uncertain what to do about his prisoner's involvement with the two men.

Ian turned back to Carol, waiting for her answer to Mark's question.

"She wanted to use me."

"Use you how?" Ian asked her.

"She had no intention of telling the whole story about feeding the world's people. She just didn't want either abortion or contraception in the world. And she wanted me to write the same thing. I did it for you."

Ian just looked at her, his face a tragic mask at Carol's pitiable confusion. She had once accused him, too, of using her, and she had flung herself from his bed in a rage. Had she murdered Mary in just such a rage, or had she killed her for some obscure idea that Mary was a threat to him? Or for both reasons?

"Mary never wanted to hurt me," he pleaded with her. "And you didn't have to write with her if you didn't want to."

"She did. She did! She wanted your work stopped. If I had refused to collaborate with her she would have told everyone you were sabotaging your own work. That you had no intention of finding solutions to the population control problems."

"She told you that?"

"Not exactly. But I knew that's what she meant. Isn't that why *you* were so good to her? She was a terrible person. She was not your friend."

Clearly Ian did not believe her but Janet was more inclined to think that much of Carol's perception of Mary was probably accurate. Ian, however, did have his blind spot. Maybe if he had the opportunity to talk awhile to Mark about it he'd get some corroboration of Carol's evaluation of his late friend.

Mark leaned against the wall as if his legs could no longer support him. He looked dreadfully ill. Almost *he* had been the one to kill Mary. Was that the reason for his appearance—the realization that he might now be in Carol's place if his plot had succeeded? Or was it remorse at what he had almost done?

"And Dr. Hu?" Ian asked. "Why Dr. Hu?"

An odd look came over Carol's face, transforming its beauty. A small, superior smile played about her lips and there was a slyness in the sideward tilt of her head as she looked at him. "You are so naive, Ian. The brilliant Dr. Chen doesn't know his little Chinese helpmate wanted to help him right into her bed. And I wouldn't be surprised if Mary wanted that too." Suddenly the slyness was gone and she looked vulnerable, defenseless. "It was all for you, Ian. I did it to protect you. You're safe now."

On Thursday Janet received word from the Ministry of Education that everything was ready for her trip to Huhehot. In an hour she was packed and ready to leave, waiting for the car and chauffeur. Fortunately they had booked her on an evening flight, so there was opportunity to say goodbye to some of the people she had met during her stay at the Friendship Hotel. The message that had been delivered by Wang Qu Qing informed her that administrators and some teachers from the college would drive with her to the airport.

Dorothy came in from work, and Janet went to say goodbye to her and John.

"Oh, dear," Dorothy moaned. "John is leaving tomorrow, and now you too."

"I wish I could stay," John said. "I dread that first day of arriving home. That first day takes it out of me; I can't sleep for twenty-four hours. All keyed up."

Janet gasped. "Did you come out of your room at six o'clock on the morning of the murder?"

"Probably. I wander a lot until I can settle down. Why?"

"Oh, nothing much. It's just that for a while you helped add to the confusion."

"Huh?"

"Nothing. Nothing at all. It's over now."

"Yes—and now I'll be all alone!"

"Nonsense," John drawled. "You draw people like flies, Dot. You're never all alone."

She sniffed.

"I'll miss you, Dorothy. Do you think you might get to Inner Mongolia any time soon?"

"Maybe. I have a vacation coming up."

"You said you'd come to Japan," John protested. And they all laughed. The world was not so big—and everyone wanted Dorothy.

"Poor Carol," Dorothy said after a while. "So beautiful—and so . . . so . . . When will she be going back to the States?"

"Soon. Ian Chen is traveling with her."

"He really loves her, doesn't he?"

"I think he does. It will be a long time before she's well. If she ever is."

"Who would have thought . . ."

"You all had that Algerian pegged for it, didn't you?"

"John Peter, you can just drop the superior pose! You thought he was odd too. And if I remember, you suggested he might have been the murderer."

"Well, he *was* odd. And running when Dr. Hu was attacked. What would anyone think?"

Janet remembered those awful white boots of Armand's that had pierced the dimness of the stores basement. It had been so easy to conjecture that the long white coat had covered the blood he must have got on his clothes when he killed Mary. But of course, she realized now, if his clothes had been splattered, his boots would have been too. And it was clear there had been nothing on his boots but the accumulated grime of Beijing.

Then why had he run after delivering the unconscious Dr. Hu to the clinic?

Poor man, she thought. Unhappy man. Looking for some way to assert a power he never had. Power that had been needed in his beloved Algeria.

No, she reproved herself. Prejudice has nothing to do with love of country. He wanted a life where dark-skinned people were his prescribed inferiors, where he would never have to prove that they were more inferior than he was.

Still—poor man. Poor everybody who needs a race to look down on in order to feel worthwhile.

"Well, time to go. If you'll give me a hand with my bags, I'll wait downstairs for the car."

She closed the door of her rooms behind her with a slight pang. It was never easy to leave a home and head for an unknown situation. She knew that once she had settled down to work in the new university she would feel very much at home there, but for the moment she was a little nervous.

The officer came out of the clinic as they stood out front smiling at each other, promising to write.

"You are leaving," he said.

"Yes."

"How fortunate that you were here to provide the vital clue."

"That's generous of you. But I think the answer would have come to you sooner or later."

"Not a happy solution," he said.

"No. And some questions still unanswered. I wonder, could Armand have known that Carol killed Mary? Is that what his threat implied?"

"I believe it is possible he knew. He was out every morning very early. It is not unlikely that he saw Miss Walker go into Mrs. Allen's hotel."

"And saw her come out again? Wearing different clothes. Maybe that's why he ran after carrying Dr. Hu to the clinic. Because he recognized Carol's handiwork again and went to warn her to leave. If that's the case, then why wouldn't he just tell the police about his suspicions? That would be a way to get her out of the country—without threats, without blackmail."

But she knew the answers to her own questions. Armand would have as little to do with the authorities as possible. And he would revel in the feeling of power over Carol, forcing her to do what *he* wanted.

Another thought occurred to her, half formed but not quite elusive. She needed to put it into words to solidify it, so it could be examined. "Some years ago I worked in a mental hospital. I believed that the patients needed a way of keeping in touch with the outside world. They were not very sick, and one day they'd be taking up their lives again. But in the hospital they were almost completely isolated. Except for family members who visited infrequently, they heard nothing about what was happening in the world.

"I had the idea of sitting with them for an hour every day in informal groups talking with them about what was happening in the community, in other countries."

"They had no radio or television?"

"No. The doctors were afraid that unmonitored newscasts and other programs might be too disturbing—that most of them wouldn't be able to handle the experience without help. And like most psychiatric hospitals, they didn't have enough qualified help to supervise the watching and listening.

"Anyhow, they accepted my idea—as long as it was *my* time I was using. What I did was clip articles and pictures from several newspapers every day and use them as a basis for discussion.

"Participation was entirely voluntary, but apparently it filled a need because the group got larger every day. The patients were really interested. Sometimes, of course, their reactions were extreme—like the time a young woman became hysterical when someone mentioned the assassination of President Kennedy, which had happened years before. But generally the discussions were quiet, intelligent, perceptive.

"One man told me that for the first time since he had become ill he felt that he was being treated as a whole person, not a patient, not an inmate of a mental hospital. Not a collection of symptoms.

"The point of this long story is that I found in the people who came to the discussions an amazing insightfulness into the emotions of others. Often they were much more sensitive and aware than the trained physicians and nurses."

Janet saw a growing understanding on the face of the officer. One lovely thing about him, he listened and understood, even though he didn't always agree. He was part of a culture that had never had serious concerns for the mentally ill, and even today the treatment emphasized getting patients to change their attitudes and be incorporated into the normal order of society. But he would hear a radical evaluation of the ability of disturbed people and not reject it out of hand.

"I think Armand may have recognized in Carol her profound disturbance. Seen her as someone at odds with society, just as he was. The patients I worked with recognized sickness in the others and, surprisingly, in themselves as well. And they never hesitated to say about someone, 'He's crazy.' The first time I heard it I was shocked, until I realized they were just stating a fact. Not insulting, not condemning. Just describing the other person's condition. And it was understandable in a way that all the medical and psychiatric labels never were. Once I could accept the simple observation, I could relate to crazy people as real people, not as collections of 'disease entities' that only served to obscure who they were."

"You think the Algerian wanted to protect Miss Walker?"

"In a way. He wanted her to get out before she was discovered, before her own craziness betrayed her."

"Perhaps one day she will reveal the whole story of what happened between them."

"You know, every day I'm more impressed with the liberality of the Chinese people. If a Chinese national had done something like this in my country, she would have had to stand trial or receive treatment in America. They would never have let her be taken home for treatment."

"It seemed the most practical solution. To be treated for severe mental illness in a foreign setting, where few people speak her language, where the food and customs are unfamiliar—it would be difficult to help her."

"Such a *civilized* decision."

He grinned. "Must I remind you again, my friend, that we are the oldest continuing civilization in the world?"

"I remember." She grinned back at him. "My surprise is not that you're capable of civilized decisions but that any human beings can rise so magnificently above all the prejudices that accompany civilization."

They were halfway to the airport—Mr. Ching, the chairman of the Department of Foreign Languages, Mr. Cai, the principal, Janet's old friend Mrs. Hua and of course Wang Qu Qing—all smiling and nodding to each other because they had run out of goodbyes and good wishes—before Janet remembered that she still didn't know the officer's name.

Charlotte Epstein is a former human relations professor, and she has written ten books and several dozen articles in that field. As Social Scientist for the Philadelphia police department she instituted a new method of police training in human relations. Like her heroine, Dr. Epstein spent a year in Beijing teaching English to scientists. MURDER AT THE FRIENDSHIP HOTEL is her second book for the Crime Club.